What readers say about Harlequin Romances

"Your books are the best I have ever found."
  P.B.*, Bellevue, Washington

"I enjoy them more and more
with each passing year."
  J.L., Spurlockville, West Virginia

"No matter how full and happy life might be,
it is an enchantment to sit
and read your novels."
  D.K., Willowdale, Ontario

"I firmly believe that Harlequin Romances
are perfect for anyone who wants to read
a good romance."
  C.R., Akron, Ohio

*Names available on request

OTHER
Harlequin Romances
by JANE DONNELLY

Dear Caliban

by

JANE DONNELLY

Harlequin Books

TORONTO • LONDON • NEW YORK • AMSTERDAM • SYDNEY

Original hardcover edition published in 1977
by Mills & Boon Limited

ISBN 0-373-02090-2

Harlequin edition published August 1977

Printed in Canada

CHAPTER ONE

ABIGAIL Lansing sat on the low sea wall and watched the man rowing in, the sunlight glinting on his brown hair and brown arms. He handled the oars with lazy skill, bringing the dinghy swiftly through the colourful fleet of bobbing boats and buoys into the shallow waters of a shelving beach.

He was a stranger to Abigail, but when she'd seen him climbing down from the magnificent power ketch that was anchored out there she had been just about to row out to it herself. They could well have met half way across, and shouting over the waves would have been awkward. It should be easier on dry land.

There were plenty of people around. St Columb's Cove had grown from a sleepy Cornish fishing village into a holiday resort without losing its character. Most of the cottages took in guests now, the two pubs were small hotels and the shops were stocked for tourists, but it was still a fishing village. The weather was good this morning and there were more pleasure boats than fishing smacks in the harbour.

Abigail had lived here for the twenty-two years of her life. She was a tall quiet girl, with nothing spectacular about her. Her features were regular, her smooth beige hair was shining and beautifully cut. She looked grave, and older than her age. Wearing a sleeveless dress of pale blue silk, and matching pale blue flat-heeled shoes, she could have been a holidaymaker. One with money. The doeskin shoes were expensive, and an impractical colour.

She sat on the sea wall, waiting until the man had secured the boat to a bollard, before she walked along to intercept him. He wore no shirt, his skin was tanned mahogany colour, coarse hair curled on his chest. Trouser legs were rolled up and he was barefoot. He looked like a fisherman, lean and hard-muscled, and when she said 'Mr Routlege?' he stopped and looked at her with narrowing eyes.

'Yes?'

'I'm——' she swallowed and tried again, 'I'm from the local newspaper, the *Penrann Telegraph*. I believe you're looking for a house around here?'

'Do you have a house to sell?' His voice was clipped, curt and unfriendly.

'No,' she said quietly, 'I just wanted to talk to you.'

'Did you?' He sounded as though he disliked the press, and some of the stories about him had made the headlines. He was a writer by trade, with a knack of stirring things both in his work and his way of life, but Abigail wasn't likely to write anything controversial about him. Her celebrity spot for the *Penrann Telegraph* was always complimentary. She only had the job because her father was a famous actor, and most of the personalities she interviewed were his friends.

But this morning the features editor had phoned her and said, 'Max Routlege's boat is in your harbour. He's been looking over some properties around here. You might try to get a chat with him before he ups anchor.' So she had come down to the sea-front and borrowed a skiff to take her alongside the ketch, when she had seen the man she was almost sure was Routlege.

Now he said, 'Excuse me, I'm busy,' and strode off, and a real reporter would have followed him, but Abbie bit her lip and stayed where she was. If she had followed he might have said something cutting and savage—he looked more than capable of it—and why should she lay herself open to insult? If Max Routlege snarled, 'Drop dead!' at her it was unlikely the *Tele-*

graph would consider that a quote for publication.

She watched the lean rangy figure, moving as easily and as purposefully through the holidaymakers as he had steered the dinghy, until he vanished down one of the side streets from the harbour to the main road.

Then she turned back to look again at the white boat, shading her eyes. Her father wasn't fond of sailing. He preferred planes for transport, and messing about in boats was not his style. So they didn't have a boat. When she went sailing she was a passenger, but invitations were never lacking for Leo Lansing's daughter.

For her first ten years Abbie had been Leo Lansing and Helen Lurie's daughter. Although her mother had died in a car crash before Abbie's second birthday people still remembered the young actress, with her silver beauty and golden promise. But she had been a theatre star, there were no films to keep her memory alive, while over the years Leo Lansing had become an international household name.

Now Abbie was 'Leo Lansing's daughter'. His only child—he had never married again—the girl he called his princess. When she met anyone who didn't know her father personally they all wanted to ask her about him, and there was no one she would rather talk about. Certainly not about herself. She didn't believe that she was interesting in any way, but her father had no more devoted fan than his daughter.

There was no need for her to hurry back home this morning, and she took her time, stopping to chat with the locals who were on the quayside. They all liked Abigail Lansing, she had grown up here and she was a nice girl.

She attracted no particular attention from the holidaymakers. Although she had appeared on publicity photographs with her father she didn't take a memorable picture. Sometimes men eyed her appreciatively, but there were plenty of other girls around, looking more provocative, more promising.

She went into the chemists to buy some sun-block cream, she freckled without it, and the lady behind the counter said, 'Hello, Abigail, another lovely day.'

'What a summer we're having,' said Abbie. As she left the shop she knew that Mrs Pinner was telling her other customers, 'That's Leo Lansing the actor's daughter. He lives near here.' She felt them looking at her through the open shop door, seeking for a resemblance to her father. Older ones, who might remember her mother, might catch something they recognised, but not much. There would be much talk about Leo Lansing's films, or one of his television appearances. They would all have heard of him, and they would be intrigued by a glimpse of his daughter.

She climbed the steep hill from the harbour, stepping aside for the cars, then she walked the cliff top path to the next cove and her home. The house was a palatial modern building, standing behind high hedges and closed gates, on the site of an old cottage her father had bought the year she was born.

She couldn't remember the cottage because Leo Lansing had been a success in his profession from the start, and demolition and rebuilding had started as soon as he bought the place. He called his new house Players' Court, which was apt enough as Leo Lansing was already being nicknamed 'King' Leo. 'Queen' Helen died, but Abbie grew up here as King Leo's princess, with a nanny in her early days, with a governess until she was seventeen.

Maudie, who had been her mother's dresser in the theatre, had always been the housekeeper. There was Ben the gardener, and a procession of domestic 'helps', mostly hoping that working for Leo Lansing might provide their break into the world of acting. It never did, and after a while they would leave disgruntled.

8

The seven-bedroomed house, usually filled with guests when Leo was in residence, ran smoothly. The food was always excellent and so was the service. But that was in spite of the domestic 'helps' rather than because of them, and Maudie had arthritis that almost crippled her at times but had to be kept from Leo because he hated illness or depression around him. So far as his own health went he was a near-hypochondriac, but he had no patience with anyone else's ailments.

The house was so well run because Abbie worked like a beaver, cleaning, cooking. She helped Maudie with the accounts, she organised the upkeep of the place, seeing that repairs and decorating were always done when her father was away. He couldn't stand anything that distracted him, from the part he was learning or the holiday he was taking.

It was good publicity that he adored his daughter, and he certainly lavished material things on her. He would have been furious to learn that she scrubbed floors and peeled potatoes. Maudie might have found herself out of a job if he had realised she was no longer physically capable of keeping the big house bandbox-neat.

So Abbie worked behind the scenes, and even the drama school hopefuls who came and went had no real idea how much she actually did. Nor did the guests, her father's friends and colleagues. They liked Abbie, who was always here to welcome them, but none of them saw her as a person in her own right. Just as a girl without ambitions, who led a very pleasant life as Leo Lansing's darling daughter, his pampered princess. It was in fact Abbie who did the pampering. Her life was lived around her father, who was a brilliant actor and a complete egotist, selfish to the core.

He was sitting by the swimming pool, alone for once, when she walked round from the driveway to the rear of the house. There were three guests staying at the moment, a celebrated surgeon and his wife, and an actress who would be appearing with Leo in his next film. But now Leo Lansing sat alone, a non-alcoholic drink at his elbow; he was watching his diet, although his torso in swimming trunks was still a youngish man's, so long as he remembered to hold in his stomach.

He smiled when he saw Abbie. He was tall and dark, and women had been mooning over his matinée-idol looks for the last twenty years. There wasn't a grey hair on his head, nor a wrinkle that couldn't pass for a laugh line.

'Where are they all?' asked Abbie. They had been sitting over breakfast when she left the house. Her father shrugged.

'Corinne went to find a hairdresser. John and Diane ran her into Penrann. They'll be back for lunch.'

It would be a light salad lunch, the weather was too warm for much else midday, and then Abbie would help Maudie prepare tonight's meal. Audrey, their current help, was more use than usual, a local girl who was impressed by the glittering company but who up to now had revealed no show business aspirations.

Maudie's arthritis wasn't too bad today, she would be coping with the lunch, and before she went in to give a hand, Abbie, feeling hot and sticky after her hill climb, stripped off her dress, revealing a white bikini, kicked off her shoes, and dived into the blue pool.

The cool water brought her tinglingly alive, as she swam with smooth strong strokes. This was bliss, she was a first-class swimmer, but when her father dived in too and called boyishly, 'Race you a couple of lengths!' she deliberately checked her pace. If she had gone full stretch she could have beaten him, and he would have hated that.

He touched the side comfortably ahead. Not even when she was a child had it once occurred to him that he might let Abbie win. He had to come in first, he must always be the star. She climbed out, smooth skin dripping, and left him doing a stylish crawl.

'There are some letters on my desk,' he called after her.

'I'll see to them,' she assured him.

The book of the film he was starting next week was beside his drink. He would have read it through and through, as closely as his script. He never turned in a performance that was less than excellent, and Abbie glanced down proudly at the best-seller that would be a sure box-office hit with her father in the leading role.

The house was cool inside, blinds drawn against the sun. The furnishings combined best modern with good period—it was a rich man's house—and the picture with pride of place, over the white marble fireplace in the drawing room, was Helen as Juliet, in a plain white gown with pearls in her smooth golden hair.

Helen and Leo had played the star-crossed lovers at Stratford-on-Avon the year they married, and their beauty and talent had brought them instant fame. Helen only had three more years to live, but Leo had gone from strength to strength.

If Abbie resembled either of her parents it was her mother. She had Helen's pale face, but her hair was a darker shade, her mouth was wider, her chin squarer. She missed Helen Lurie's breathtaking beauty, and her exquisite fragility. Abbie was taller, possibly stronger, although Maudie told tales of Helen's iron determination to reach the top, a dedication equal to Leo's.

Abbie was as proud of her mother's memory as she was of her father. She had had incredibly talented parents and it was unlucky that she hadn't inherited much talent herself. She had wanted to go to drama school, but her father had put a stop to that, telling her flatly that she was without the spark of genius, and anything less would be hell for her. As his daughter she might get the initial breaks, but the critics would tear her apart. She accepted his judgment—he knew, of course—and now seven years later she was devoting her life to him.

She watched his diet, she saw that he took his vitamin pills, she worried over the heart condition that was a closely kept secret but meant he must avoid worry and stress. He was the pivot of her existence. She doubted if there was another man to equal her father.

She had had several near-affairs, she met some very attractive young men in her father's orbit, but so far nothing had come of them. There was a young man now whom she liked very much and she was hoping that this time the relationship would not fizzle out.

Mostly she presumed that when anyone began to know her well they found she wasn't what they'd expected. She lacked the spark; they hadn't realised that Leo Lansing and Helen Lurie's daughter could be ordinary. It was depressing when admirers lost interest, one time it almost broke her heart, but her father always laughed and said they weren't right for her, and bought her something splendid to console her.

She had a fantastic collection of jewellery, every piece noted by the gossip columnists, and when her father was here she wore the jewellery in the evenings, keeping it in a wall safe. When he wasn't around it stayed in the bank. She didn't really want all this costly stuff, she would have loved to buy junk jewellery sometimes and wear it for fun instead of having to insure it.

Her clothes too. She had a wardrobe full of model dresses, because she was Leo Lansing's daughter and that was how he wanted her dressed. He had once smiled at her and said, 'You're never going to be beautiful, my princess, but so long as you're wearing beautiful things they'll never know.'

That was when she was accompanying him to the first night of one of his films. She had been just seventeen, emerging from the schoolroom and desperately anxious not to let him down in any way.

She never had. He called her his princess, and she dressed the part, and of course it was wonderful to have everything she wanted. She had no idea how skilfully he had nipped those near-affairs in the bud. He had a role for Abbie to play, looking after him for the rest of her life.

Upstairs Audrey was finishing the bedrooms. She was a solidly built girl with long straight hair. She moved dreamily but doggedly through her tasks, and thought Abbie was one of the luckiest girls alive. Carrying her dress, wet from the swimming pool, Abbie stopped to talk to her for a moment or two.

Abigail Lansing had no side on her, she was interested in you—Audrey gave her that, asking now about the dance Audrey had been to last night, if she'd enjoyed herself. Audrey's young man worked in the marine yard and he was all right, but the men Abigail Lansing met were out of this world, like her clothes, like this house. Audrey stood, sighing enviously, the vacuum cleaner whirring away on one spot, as Abbie went off in the direction of her own bedroom.

Abbie's room didn't get the morning treatment. 'Miss Abigail likes to see to her own room,' Maudie had always told the helps. All the housework Abbie did was done unobtrusively to keep up this illusion that Abbie was a lady of leisure. When her father wasn't around she pitched in more obviously, although it was always supposed to be Maudie who was in charge and carrying the load.

Abbie got out of her wet bikini, showered swiftly and dressed again. She looked in on Maudie in the kitchen before she went to the study where the letters were waiting for her on her father's desk.

Maudie was a small cockney sparrow, skinny-legged, sharp-featured. She had been a super-efficient housekeeper here until the arthritis began to slow her down. It started about the time Abbie finished her schooling, and without Abbie's support Maudie knew that Leo would soon have noticed and she would have been out, pensioned off somewhere. She had been with Helen almost from drama school, and running this house since Helen died, but Leo Lansing would have said, 'Well done, thou good and faithful servant,' with a theatrical catch in his voice, and never cared if he never saw her again.

Maudie knew how self-centred Leo was. Helen had been the same. They both had the obsession with themselves that is probably inborn in every great actor and actress. Maudie had adored Helen, she adored Leo. But she loved Abbie, she passed sleepless nights worrying about Abbie.

She was the only one who knew what Leo Lansing's professed devotion to his daughter was costing Abigail. No life of her own, always revolving around him like a small planet around the sun.

He hadn't married again, because he hadn't needed to. He was famous, there were always women available for him, and there was Abbie to act as nurse, secretary, hostess. The money he spent on Abbie stayed in the family. If he put jewels on a new wife or a girl-friend he might lose them, but not when he gave them to Abbie.

Maudie also knew there was no way she could make Abbie see this. So she worried, and discussed it with nobody, except sometimes a word or two with Ben. Who was going to agree with them that Leo Lansing— charming, popular, possibly an actor of genius and probably due to be knighted soon—was also a bit of a monster?

'Hello, chicken,' said Maudie as Abbie walked into the kitchen. 'Did you get to see the feller?'

'I saw him.' Maudie was sitting at the kitchen table, preparing salad side dishes, and Abbie picked out a radish. 'But he wouldn't talk to me,' she said as she nibbled. 'I don't think he likes the press.'

'Another bighead,' sighed Maudie. Abbie laughed.

'What do you mean—another?' although almost everyone who came to this house seemed to have an inflated opinion of themselves. They were all near the top of their professions, so maybe they had reason.

'He's looking at property round here,' Abbie went on. 'If he finds anything I hope it isn't too near,' and Maudie looked out over the cliff top that had been groomed into velvet lawns and flower beds. With the high walls and fencing this house was almost shut off from the outside world. The nearest building was ten minutes' brisk walk away.

'Who could get close to this place unless they were asked in?' said Maudie.

'We won't ask him,' said Abbie. 'He was a grouch. I'm just going along to the study to see to the letters.'

She handled none of her father's official business, but the fan letters that came for him all received a personal reply. And that was Abbie. She often signed them in her father's hand, when he was busy or bored. He had a reputation for caring about his fans, but in fact it was Abbie who answered their questions, and sent them photographs.

She enjoyed it. Anyone who wrote to say how thrilled and moved they had been by her father's acting was a friend of hers. When the letters were typed she put them in the folder in the top drawer of the desk, so that her father could glance through them before they were mailed. And then she phoned the *Penrann Telegraph*.

'Sorry,' she told the editor, 'but all he said was, "Excuse me, I'm busy".'

'Was he busy?'

'He meant he wasn't giving me an interview.'

'Did you tell him who you were?'

That she was Leo Lansing's daughter. 'No,' she said,

although it was her Open Sesame to most things, and when the editor suggested,

'Would your father ask him up to the house?' she bit her lip.

Max Routlege was very successful. He wrote hard and lived hard. Her father would invite him up here if Abbie wanted him invited, and Routlege would probably come. He wasn't anti-social, he mixed, he liked company. Barring reporters, it seemed.

She said, 'You really want an article about him?' and the editor sounded weary.

'He's got a series running on television that's topping the ratings, and he's looking for a local house, that gives him local colour. Yes, of course we want something about him.'

'Of course,' echoed Abbie. 'Yes, all right, then, I'll do that.'

Once he was up here she could apologise, and ask the sort of questions no one could find offensive, like what sort of house was he looking for, what was he working on at the moment. But she didn't want to have to talk to him at all, because his boorish brush-off down at the harbour just now had seemed so personal. Maybe his contempt was for the press in general, but he had looked at her as though she had crawled from under a stone, and he disliked every blessed single thing about her.

The visitors returned for lunch from their trip into town. John Wesson was a surgeon, Diane was his wife. Corinne Comer was the actress who would be playing a sultry charmer opposite Leo in a week's time, and Abbie joined them on the terrace where they were sipping cool drinks. The women had had their hair done this morning, and were both quite pleased with the results.

Abbie admired Diane's neat sleek red head, and Corinne's dark thick toss of curls, topped up everybody's glass, poured herself a tonic water with crushed ice, and asked her father, 'Do you know Max Routlege?'

'I've met him. Why?'

'His boat's down there. I tried to get an interview with him this morning, but he wouldn't be interviewed. So I wondered if you'd ask him to dinner.'

Dianne and John looked surprised. They hadn't realised that Abbie was a journalist, and Leo explained with smiling condescension, 'Abbie sometimes does little pieces for the local rag.'

'Max Routlege?' squealed Corinne ecstatically. 'The man I'd most like to be marooned on a desert island with! I'd love to meet him.' She amended that hastily to 'one of the men' because publicity was linking her with Leo, off set as well as on, for this film. That was why she was down here, and as an up-and-coming actress she had a tremendous admiration for Leo Lansing.

John Wessen said, 'He's a fine writer.'

'He might not come,' said Abbie. She couldn't easily have explained her feelings, but it was as though she hadn't just irritated him this morning, she had angered him so that he might turn dangerously on her. She was apprehensive, although she couldn't have said why.

If he refused her father's invitation that was it. If he came she would probably get a chatty little piece for the *Telegraph*. Either way it wasn't that important, so why did she have this nagging suspicion that she would do better to leave Max Routlege alone? He could hardly snub her in her father's house, and if he did why should it bother her?

'I'll send him a note,' said her father.

Ben went down to the harbour and delivered a note, and came back with the reply that Max Routlege would be delighted to join Leo Lansing for dinner, and looked forward to seeing him around seven o'clock this evening.

17

Abbie had had a date for this evening. Now she had to phone and suggest that Bryan came over here instead of taking her out.

Bryan Gibson was a TV cameraman whom she had met at a party a few weeks ago. Abbie was wary of letting herself care too quickly because she had been badly hurt once. She had been falling in love, sure that Stephen felt the same way, and then it happened like the others, he had lost interest and moved out of her life.

But she enjoyed Bryan's company. He was attentive and attractive, and—well, she really liked him and he liked her, and maybe it would go on from there.

He came to the phone and sounded disappointed when she started, 'About tonight, I'm afraid——'

'Oh no!' he said, but when she explained the situation he cheered up. Like everyone she knew he was an admirer of her father's work, and he knew Max Routlege by reputation and was very willing to spend the evening with them. And with Abbie, of course.

No one asked where Abbie spent the afternoon. Her father and his guests passed it sunbathing around the pool, and Abbie was in the kitchen, preparing tonight's meal while Maudie took a rest.

It was a crazy thing, that her father didn't even realise that Abbie could cook. Maudie had taught her for fun in the old days, when Abbie was a child and her father's visits to the house were fewer. Abbie lived for his coming, but there were long stretches between and learning to be a first-class cook was one of the ways Abbie passed her time. Now she was a better cook than Maudie, although when the meals were served it was taken for granted that Maudie had prepared them.

Audrey couldn't quite understand this, and Abbie explained, 'Maudie isn't as young as she was and I've got time to spare.'

The evening was almost as warm as the day had

18

been, with the heaviness of thunder in the air. Although the windows were opened wide the atmosphere inside was breathless.

Abbie dressed carefully, choosing another blue dress. She had a lot of blue in her wardrobe—her mother's eyes had been the most beautiful blue. Abbie's eyes were a blue-green, but she wore a lot of blue. This dress was long and had a single shoulder strap, leaving one smooth white shoulder bare. She clipped on diamond studded ear-rings the shape of small hearts, matching the flashing rings on her fingers.

Her make-up was pale, pearl-like. On this sultry evening she looked cool, and of course she wasn't nervous about meeting Max Routlege again. She stood at the dressing table, for some reason remembering her father say, 'You're never going to be beautiful, but so long as you dress beautifully no one will know,' and told her reflection, 'You may not be beautiful, but you certainly look expensive.'

She wondered how Max Routlege would dress for this visit. Hardly as she had seen him this morning, of course. She tried to imagine him conservatively clad, but the picture of him shirtless and barefooted was firm in her mind. He might put on better manners with more clothes. He could be a different character entirely.

Maybe she wouldn't recognise him, nor he her. But she would have to admit that she wanted some of their table talk for a newspaper paragraph, and although he hadn't looked at her for long he had looked piercingly. He'd remember all right, and he might be annoyed at her trick to get him here and talking.

'Blow the man,' she thought. 'If he turns round and goes home without his dinner I've done all I can.' She almost hoped he would.

She went into the kitchen to check that all was going smoothly there. The cold cucumber soup was well chilled—her father's portion to be served with the merest suggestion of a cream whorl. Then veal cutlets, and finally melon sorbet spiced with dry sherry. Audrey had gone home, but Maudie was managing.

'Keep away from the oven,' Maudie advised. 'You don't want to get anything down that dress.'

In the drawing room her father was entertaining his guests with stories that Abbie had heard many times before. He played half a dozen parts in as many minutes, and his audience was hooked. Abbie enjoyed the performance, although it was familiar to her. She sat on the arm of a chair and listened as delightedly as the other three, until the doorbell rang.

'I'll get it,' she said, 'it's probably Bryan.' It would take Maudie a few minutes to get along to the front door, and it probably was Bryan. Even if it was Max Routlege she had to face him so she might as well get it over with.

The front door was open. Bryan stood waiting for someone to tell him to step in, looking handsome and discreetly trendy, and carrying flowers in pink tissue paper.

'For me?' Abbie was pleased, although she thought how silly that sounded. Bryan would hardly be bringing her father freesias, much though he admired him. She said, 'Thank you very much, I'll put them in water right away.'

There were three Chinese vases on a long black carved Chinese chest in the hall. She put the freesias on the table, and took one of the vases into the cloakroom to fill it with water, asking Bryan as she did how his day had gone.

He told her about the programme he had been working on, filming three councillors who were a committee on a rates problem. 'Very dull,' he said. 'I've been looking forward to this evening all day.'

'I hope it doesn't disappoint you.' She began to arrange her flowers.

'That's not likely.' The food would be good and her father would keep the conversation sparkling, but Abbie grimaced.

'Have you ever met Max Routlege?'

'Not personally, I haven't.'

'Well, I met him for half a minute this morning, as I told you, and he was heavy going. I'm just praying he'll sing for his supper.'

Her head was bowed over the freesias, but she heard Bryan mutter something and looked up and round to see Max Routlege in the doorway. He must have heard. He had heard, because as she stood there, holding a spray of freesia and gasping, he came into the hall towards her, and asked, 'What tune did you have in mind?'

He recognised her. He gave her the same hard level stare she had got down on the beach, and when she stammered, 'This must be rather a surprise,' he said cynically,

'There isn't much you could do that I'd find surprising, Miss Lansing.'

So he had known who she was all along. And disliked her. And why, for goodness' sake, when she'd never done him any harm? He sounded as though she was a bore, incapable of surprising, an utterly predictable female.

Beside her Bryan shuffled and she said, 'Bryan Gibson, Max Routlege. Be a darling, Bryan, and take Mr Routlege in to the others while I finish arranging my flowers.'

'Your wish is my command,' said Bryan fervently.

'It would be,' said Max Routlege.

The fragrance of freesias was a perfume she loved, they were such delicately beautiful flowers. But now she was arranging them blindly, even the scent wasn't reaching her. It was a new experience for her to meet someone who showed they disliked her. Her father's reputation put up a little force field around her, keeping out the cold. Everyone smiled on Leo Lansing's daughter. He was the king, and she was his princess.

The gossip columns sometimes reported her unlucky love life, but her father would remind her that they spied on his private life too, and what did it matter so long as the public still raved about his work? They might write, 'Sympathies once again to Abigail, blonde twenty-two-year-old daughter of Leo Lansing, as yet another of her promising romances seems to have died the death.' But who cared what they wrote when Abbie's heart had never been involved?

Except with Stephen. And no one suspected that she had suffered for Stephen.

She went into the kitchen to tell Maudie the guests were all here, and to pass a little more time before she went back into the drawing room. So Max Routlege didn't like her. Well, she didn't like him, so that evened things up. She slipped silently into the drawing room, and stood watching the little group around the empty fireplace, under the painting of Helen as Juliet.

In spite of the heat of the evening Leo was wearing a midnight-blue velvet suit, with one of the frilled shirts he wore like a Regency rake. He was sitting in the biggest chair, giving a grand performance.

Max Routlege wore a lightweight grey suit, a grey shirt, a tie in grey knitted silk. In shadow colours he should have merged into the background, but he didn't. Even Leo's performance was being prompted by Routlege's questions and comments.

Perhaps she was being jaundiced and Max Routlege was just enjoying their company. They enjoyed his. Around the dinner table their talk covered the world.

Leo Lansing had filmed or acted or travelled to most countries. Max Routlege had been a wanderer all his adult life. Everybody had something to contribute to the conversation, except Abbie. She had travelled, usually with her father, but Max Routlege made her feel useless when she admitted that she had gone along for fun, not because she had been part of the team. She had looked after her father, but nobody knew that, and from the way Max Routlege surveyed her he thought her life was one long pleasure trip and she wouldn't know how to start earning her passage.

He was interested in Corinne's career. He had seen —or said he had—the two films she had made. He appeared impressed with John, appreciative of Diane's role as a top surgeon's wife. He discussed TV filming with Bryan. And of course he was bowled over—or seemed to be—by that great actor Leo Lansing.

But he passed over Abbie as though she was one of the candelabra, registering the glitter, and then taking no further notice. When she said, as they finished their main course, 'Would you object to me writing that you had dinner with us, Mr Routlege?' he asked,

'How could I?'

Maudie had rounded the table, depositing the sorbet dishes, and everyone picked up their spoons.

'I write what's called a celebrity column for the *Penrann Telegraph*,' Abbie explained. 'Nothing that isn't complimentary. No one gets knocked. It's more a free ad.'

'My publishers handle my publicity,' he said gravely.

Somebody certainly did. His exploits got coverage. Coming in among the leaders in Atlantic races, climbing to the twenty-thousand-foot summit of Mount Mc-Kinley in Alaska. Not to mention his ex-girl-friends and currently a much-married titled lady. And his books and plays, of course.

Abbie looked down at her sorbet, in case he could read her expression as plainly as she seemed to be reading his, and asked sweetly, 'You're thinking about buying a house round here?'

'I've been looking at property.'

'What kind of house? Do you mind being asked what kind?'

This morning he had minded being spoken to, but perhaps she had disturbed a train of creative thought, or he had got out of his bunk on the wrong side. This evening he said, 'Near the sea, not too large.'

'That sounds like your boat,' she murmured, and remembering the *Cormorant* she went on impulsively, 'It looked absolutely beautiful.'

He grinned. 'If you ever want a job as a deckhand let me know.'

They all laughed. Abbie, in her diamonds and her model gown, her healthy skin pale and perfect under a veil of cosmetics, looked an unlikely deckhand.

'What *do* you do with your time, Miss Lansing?' asked Max Routlege, adding ironically, 'Apart from your celebrity spot for the *Penrann Telegraph*.'

'The name is Abigail,' said her father. Only Maudie and Ben ever called her Abbie. 'I'm an old-fashioned father,' said Leo, smiling at her. 'I believe the girl's place is in the home.' His smile became sad and remote, looking into long distances, away from the faces around his table. 'Not Helen, of course,' he said. 'She had a gift that transcended everything.' Although he would have been indignant if anyone had suggested, even now, that his late wife was as talented an actress as he was an actor.

His gaze came back to Abbie. 'My princess,' he said huskily, 'has her kingdom here.' He meant where he was, and although it sounded highly theatrical only Max Routlege hid a smile. Abbie said lightly,

'Unlike my mother I have no special gifts.'

'No?' Max Routlege's eyes flickered around her diamonds and she said,

'No special talents, I should have said.'

She had gifts galore, and she knew exactly what he thought of her, that she was spoiled and useless. Her father and Bryan shook their heads and smiled. They didn't mean she had talents, but they were both indicating that they were satisfied with her doing nothing except looking pretty.

'Such modesty,' drawled Max Routlege. She might have said, 'Talking of talents, I'm a smashing cook. Pity I can't take a bow for the nice things that have been said about the food.'

She asked them all, 'Do you like the sorbet?'

'It's delicious,' said Dianne quickly, seizing the chance to change the subject. Max Routlege was baiting Abigail, laughing at her, and no one ever did that. At least not to her face, not in front of Leo. 'You must give me the recipe.'

'That's Maudie's department,' said Leo. 'Our treasure, Maudie.' Max was the only one who didn't know about Maudie, and Leo told him, 'Maudie's been in charge of this house for over twenty years. She's a great cook, she runs the place without a hitch, she can turn her hand to anything.'

Maudie's hands were gnarled now. She was growing old, but only Abbie saw it.

'You are lucky,' said Diane. 'Getting help in the house is such a problem these days.' But before she could start on her domestic problems Leo was reminiscing about some of the stage-struck 'help' they had had, playing all the parts again.

He was always an affable host, he usually gave a one-man show at the dinner table, but tonight he was in top form so that when Max Routlege decided it was time to say goodnight everyone was surprised to find how late it was.

Leo shook hands with his guest, urging him to buy a house near here. 'We might get together on a play some time,' said Leo. 'How about writing a good part for me?'

A less established writer would have been overwhelmed at the suggestion, but Max Routlege was as big a name as Leo Lansing, so he was promising nothing, although he sounded as enthusiastic as his host. He turned down with thanks Bryan's offer of a lift to the harbour, preferring to walk, and Abbie went along to wave Bryan off, leaving her father and Max Routlege still talking.

'It was a fantastic evening,' said Bryan. 'Your father's a fantastic man.'

'Isn't he?' said Abbie.

The night still airless and there wasn't a cloud in the sky. Stars pierced the heavy dome of blackness and a yellow moon hung full and round. The only sound was the sea.

'Max Routlege could tell some tales too,' said Brian. 'Some of his would make your hair stand on end.'

'He writes them,' said Abbie. 'That way he gets paid for them.'

Bryan laughed. He supposed she was joking. They walked down from the terrace, across to his car in the driveway, and he took her in his arms. 'Goodnight,' he said, and kissed her tenderly. She was fragrant to kiss, smooth skin and smooth clothes, and she kissed him lightly back. 'Lunch tomorrow?' he said.

'Yes, please.'

She watched the car go. Her father had enjoyed this evening. They all had, except Abbie, who had felt Max Routlege's contempt every time he glanced her way, every time she spoke. He thought she was a born hanger-on, and what business would it be of his if she were? She wouldn't be hanging on to him.

She walked back to the terrace, up the wide flat steps, and stood with her hands on the cool white stone of the balustrade. The lights from the house spilled out behind her, and out here everything was breathless, as though it was waiting.

Lunch tomorrow with Bryan, and perhaps Bryan

was going to take Stephen's place. She sighed, Stephen still hurt, and as she did she felt the shadow. She didn't think she heard a footstep, but perhaps she had, because she knew who was near and she didn't turn her head. She hoped he would pass with a mere 'Good-night.' She didn't expect him to linger.

'Sighing for the moon?' he said.

'What?'

He was level with her now, looking down at her, mocking her with sham sympathy. 'It must come hard, princess, realising there are some things your father can't buy for you.'

CHAPTER TWO

'BELIEVE it or not, I never really wanted the moon.'
Abbie's voice was languid, as though she was finding
this very boring, and she managed a smile to match.
'Thank you for the interview, Mr Routlege,' she said,
'and goodnight.'

'Thank you for your hospitality,' he said dryly.

'You mean my father's hospitality.'

He shrugged, and she smiled again, with a gracious
inclination of the head as though she really was a
princess. She hoped he realised that she was sending
him up, but on that she left him, walking back into the
house, and very likely he'd think she hadn't a gleam of
humour in her.

That was what people did think, that she was a very
serious girl. It was only with Maudie and Ben that she
joked, and not in her father's hearing. Leo Lansing was
an expert at witty anecdotes but, unless they were
smiling at his wit, he liked his women quiet. Abbie
usually kept her laughter, and most of her thoughts, to
herself.

Everyone was drifting off to bed. She had put her
father's overnight pills on his bedside table with a glass
of water, and now she kissed him goodnight.

'You run along to bed, princess,' he said. 'I can't have
you missing your beauty sleep.' And in their bedroom
later Diane said to her husband,

'What a fuss Leo makes of Abigail. Max Routlege
hadn't got much time tonight for her, had he?'

'She's a nice enough girl,' said John, yawning. 'Just
doesn't have much go in her.'

In her bedroom Abbie got out of her beautiful dress

and put on a cotton housecoat that had short sleeves and buttoned neatly around her. While her father and his guests were in the house she couldn't risk getting caught in a pinafore, but this was the next best thing. She was not tired. If she had gone to bed she wouldn't have slept, but there was plenty to do before she climbed between the sheets.

She carried the coffee cups and the glasses into the kitchen and then took over the sink, finishing the remaining washing up, scouring out pans and giving the oven a quick wipe down.

'Off to bed with you,' she'd said to Maudie, planting a kiss on her cheek. Maudie had been sitting, nodding, in an armchair. This had been their routine for quite a time, that Abbie did the later-night clearing up. Maudie wasn't good for much, she admitted to Abbie and Ben and nobody else, after about eleven o'clock.

It was well after midnight now and Maudie said, 'All right, chicken,' and went up the back stairs.

Abbie laid the table in the breakfast room and flicked around the dining and drawing rooms. When everything was in order and she put out the lights the rest of the house was in darkness, and she went quietly to her own room. It was still sultry. She was glad to get out of her housecoat and she supposed she would sleep, but she decided she would write up her few lines on Max Routlege first. She would be delivering them in the morning and she certainly didn't want to start tomorrow with him on her mind.

She took the top off her little yellow portable typewriter, on the bureau desk against the wall, and tapped out a few paragraphs. Their readers would know who Max Routlege was. This television series of his was getting a massive audience, his paperbacks were on all the bookstalls, and quite often his name was in the newspapers.

She wrote a short piece, culled from what he had said

over the dinner table, that he had been looking for a house in the area where he could work in peace and entertain his friends, that he loved Cornwall, especially the coastline. She wondered whether to add that he was thinking of writing a play for Leo Lansing, but knew if that got into print he would deny it and her father would be angry. It would be lovely to disconcert Max Routlege, but not at that cost.

She yanked the second and last page from her typewriter, and for a moment considered a quick swim in the pool. Swimming was her chief way of using up surplus energy. There was almost too much energy in Abbie, sometimes it burned in her.

If she had been an actress she might have channelled this life force into imaginary characters. As it was, she did the chores, and everything she could to make life easier for her father, and swam, and passed for a quiet over-protected girl with no go in her.

She decided against creeping downstairs and into the pool. Corinne's room overlooked it and Abbie might have to explain in the morning why she was swimming up and down at two a.m.

Part of her restlessness was the sultry night, part of it was Max Routlege. He had shaken her up, and with the lights off in her room she pulled the curtains and looked out over the sea. His boat was anchored beyond the coves. She pinpointed its navigation lights and thought that it would be cooler out there, and pulled a face in his direction, remembering him saying, 'Nothing you could do would surprise me, Miss Lansing.'

It would surprise him if she added that bit about the play he didn't intend to write. Or would it? He would probably decide she had taken his reaction to her father's suggestion on its face value, that she was too thick to see he wasn't promising a thing.

But she wished, as she had never done before, that she could have asked awkward questions and produced an article that might raise eyebrows. Max Routlege's love life now, no one had gone into that around last night's dinner table. Suppose she had said, 'If you get this house will Lady Anne be moving in with you and getting her third divorce?'

That would have been equal to her emptying a bowl of soup over someone's head. So out of character that her father would have called in a psychiatrist, but she grinned, savouring it, and went back to her typewriter and fed in another sheet of paper, and did a spoof interview where she did put the question and Max Routlege said, 'We are just good friends,' and she said, 'Of course you are. Like Lady Chatterley and her gentleman caller,' and so on.

She thought it quite funny in a childish way. She wished there was someone she could show it to, for the laughs, but of course there wasn't, and she tore it into small pieces and dropped it in her wastepaper basket, and slept soundly until it was time to be up, and seeing about breakfast and the day ahead.

Thunder was rolling around the sky. A storm might lift the oppressiveness, but thundery weather played up Maudie's arthritis and she was walking stiffly round the kitchen when Abbie came down.

'Bad this morning?' asked Abbie. Maudie flexed her joints as best she could and winced.

'Giving me a bit of gyp.'

Today should be fairly easy for Maudie. Dianne and John were leaving after their week's holiday. Corinne and Leo were off to the regional TV studios to appear in a film magazine, and were staying the evening with friends. They wouldn't be back until late, and Abbie was lunching with Bryan.

Once breakfast was over Abbie got into the car, a pale blue Triumph Stag with A.L. on the number plate, her father's last birthday present to her that had brought him a lot of publicity. She drove into Penrann, found a parking space in the *Telegraph* car park, and went up to the editorial floor in the creaking old lift.

The editor's small office, like all the other offices, looked out on a central corridor through glass-panelled walls and door, and Hugh Trelawney, benign and bulky and bored with his job, raised a faint smile for Abbie when she walked in.

She said, 'I brought you something about Max Routlege, he did come to dinner last night.'

'Who'd refuse an invitation to court from King Leo?' said Hugh, and Abbie went on smiling, although there was a hint of sarcasm in his voice. He read her article and said, 'That'll do.'

'Good. Good morning, then.' She turned to go and Hugh said,

'Abigail.'

'Yes?'

Being Leo Lansing's daughter Abigail Lansing mixed with public figures, which meant she could often turn in a name-dropping paragraph and was why she had been approached last year and asked to become a social correspondent for the *Telegraph*. But she had never sent them anything that wasn't a kid glove treatment, and Hugh said now, 'I thought you might have come up with something a bit livelier about Max Routlege. He's a hell of a man, you know.'

My sentiments entirely, thought Abbie dourly, but we don't mean it the same way. She said quietly, 'I'm sorry, but the people I write about are usually our guests. I can't embarrass them.'

Hugh looked at her wearily. 'No, I'm sure you couldn't,' he said.

Abbie knew that at the first sign that her scribblings were becoming controversial her father would stop the whole thing. It never occurred to her that he couldn't forbid her to stop writing about the well-known names she met. She would never do anything to upset him.

But Max Routlege was a temptation. The only guest she would have enjoyed embarrassing. She thought, as she drove away from the *Telegraph*, that if she had known anything Max Routlege didn't want the press to know she would seriously have considered tipping off Hugh, and like a coward asking him not to disclose his source of information.

But she didn't know a thing. And she hoped this was the last time she would be bothered with Max Routlege. She wouldn't think about him buying a house in the neighbourhood and becoming a regular caller at Players' Court. That was a nasty thought, but for lots of reasons it might never happen.

She met Bryan for lunch in the best known restaurant in town. She would have preferred somewhere smaller and more intimate, where there were fewer people around whom Bryan knew. They always seemed to go to places like this. How could he offer her less than the best? he said, and she found it impossible to explain how she disliked the feeling of being on permanent display when she was with him.

She didn't want all this public fuss. She wanted privacy, a chance to talk and listen, to discover and be discovered. Perhaps, like Max Routlege, Bryan had decided she had no surprises in store for him. Perhaps if they did have quiet times together he would realise how dull she was, and leave her like the others.

She sighed deeply and Bryan asked, 'Is anything the matter?'

'It's the heat,' she said. 'It's so heavy.'

The air-conditioning was good in here, but he agreed with her. Then he said, 'Do you think we could get Max Routlege along?' and she realised that, between waving at friends and chatting with the ones who passed their table, Bryan must have been saying something to her.

'Get him where?' she asked.

'This party, on Monday night.' She did know about the party. Her father was flying to France on Monday and she was going to a party with Bryan, and he must have mentioned it just now because he sounded as though he had. His smile looked fixed, plastered over exasperation, and Abbie said quickly,

'I'm so sorry, I was daydreaming. The party—yes, of course, but what do you mean about Max Routlege?'

Bryan forgave her for daydreaming, disentangling her hand from her coffee cup and squeezing her fingers while he told her, 'Everybody would like to meet him. He's a hell of a man.'

'That seems to be the general impression,' Abbie murmured.

'So I thought you might ask him to come along?'

'Not me!' she said, more forcefully than Bryan had ever heard her react before. 'You ask him if you must, and then you count me out. I had more than enough of him last night.'

'You did?' He hadn't seen it. He really hadn't seen that Max Routlege despised her. He must have thought the sneers were good clean fun, and the way Max Routlege looked through or past her as though hers was the empty chair—well, he couldn't have noticed that at all. He was waiting now to hear why Abbie had had enough of Max Routlege, and she almost burst out laughing.

But Abigail Lansing didn't burst out laughing because something struck her as ridiculous. She never did anything as uninhibited as that. Instead she said, 'I took a dislike to him. It's hard to explain, but——' she shrugged and Bryan smiled ruefully.

'All right, forget it. You're the one I want to take to the party.' He picked up her hand again, kissing it this time, and said, 'Why didn't we go somewhere we could have been alone?'

That was an odd thing to ask as he had chosen the restaurant. 'Monday night, darling,' he said softly, 'I

34

want to talk to you very seriously.'

'You do?' He still had her hand, and they were being watched with interest by several other diners as he gave her a smouldering look, whispering,

'I'm crazy about you. Think about that, will you, between now and then?'

He settled the bill, and kissed her goodbye, putting her into her car, cursing his ill luck in having to go back to work when he would so much rather have been spending the rest of the day with her. She drove away feeling flustered, although she looked calm enough.

The car was an automatic and almost drove itself. It dealt smoothly with the holiday traffic stops and starts. Abbie was used to the admiring looks it got, and the curious ones from pedestrians and other drivers, wondering who A.L. was. Her father's number plate on his Rolls-Royce was an L.L. and he was often recognised. Nobody recognised Abbie, they just asked each other, 'Who should you think that was?'

All the way home, of course, she was wondering what she and Bryan were going to discuss so seriously as soon as they were alone. Perhaps he was going to ask her to marry him. He'd told her he was crazy about her, and asked her to think about that, so what else could it be? He wasn't likely to suggest them living together, it would take a braver man than Bryan to proposition King Leo's daughter, but their relationship seemed due for a change.

That moving on she had hoped for? Oh yes, she did want that. She wanted to be loved. Sometimes her woman's body was restless and unsatisfied, but if Bryan was her lover, her husband, then she wouldn't be afraid of rejection. She had a lack of confidence in herself, fostered by her lack of success with the men in her life. Everyone was nice to Abigail Lansing, but the men she might have loved smiled and went.

Like Stephen. It was nearly a year since she first met

Dr Stephen Faber. He was on a month's holiday down here, having just completed his medical training and passed his finals. He was sensitive, clever and kind, and Abbie saw him every day.

Her father was home that month; Players' Court was open house to a stream of guests, and they all liked Stephen. So did her father, he told her so, but one night after a party Stephen left with a glossy lady from a glossy magazine, and that was the last Abbie saw or heard of him.

It hurt her deeply because Stephen was the first man she had really longed for. She had let her dreams run riot, and although her father took her off to Paris and they had a marvellous holiday she missed Stephen badly.

She still did a little. She hadn't found anyone else with the rapport she believed she could have shared with Stephen. She was beginning to wonder if she was emotionally frigid, physically too perhaps, but then Bryan had moved in on the scene.

Bryan was crazy about her, he had just told her so, and they had something very serious to discuss. Of course she was intrigued and excited. Her father would be leaving on Monday, her life would be emptier, but perhaps what Bryan had to say to her would fill it.

No one had ever asked her to marry them before. According to her father that was because none of her transitory admirers had been the right man for her, but she was sure he would be happy if she told him she was in love at last. She really believed that he would accept as a son any man she loved.

Even if her father had been home she wouldn't have said anything to him yet. She had some thinking to do first. She wasn't crazy about Bryan. She liked him very much, but her heart didn't ache for him, as it had done for Stephen, although that wasn't to say she couldn't come to love him. There was a glow of affection in her for him, and a glow might fan into a flame. If you were careful, and blew it gently and kept it out of the wind, it might set your world on fire.

She didn't say anything to Maudie either. She took herself off to turn out the guest room that John and Diane had used, and when that was done, with the long summer evening stretching ahead, she told Maudie, 'I'm going for a walk, probably down to the harbour.'

But, out of the house, she changed her mind in favour of a swim.

The grounds of Players' Court went to the cliffs' edge, and from there precipitous footholds could take you down to a small cove far below. It wasn't used by their visitors. If you wanted to sunbathe or swim there were better facilities around the house, and better coves a little way along the coast. The rocks were sharp here, the submerged ones could be deadly, as Abbie always pointed out when guests asked her about the swimming.

The only access was from the sea or down the cliff, and you needed to be a mountaineer or a monkey to negotiate the cliff face unless you knew just where the footholds were. Abbie had always known. She had scrambled down to the cove as a child, and swum between the encircling cliffs, over the rocks out into the open sea.

Well out of the cove and the harbour there was a rock that she shared with the seagulls, where she would lie at ease, revelling in the solitude, before swimming back again.

The little cove and the craggy rock were her own private domain. Her father certainly didn't want to share them. No one did, and now, down in the cove, she took off her dress and shoes, put them on a high rock shelf in a cave and slipped into the water.

She knew where the razor rocks were, she knew the

currents. Out of the cove she could look back on the coastline and the boats in the harbour of St Columb's. She passed the *Cormorant*, and wished she had a boat like that to sail away in. Her car was lovely, but you are earthbound with a car, hemmed in. She floated, looking up at the wheeling birds and the little scudding clouds, then swam again, fast and strongly towards her rock, and reached it with an enjoyable feeling of languor.

It had a narrow beach of shingle, then a scramble up to a flat space large enough for comfortable sunbathing, and almost a cave behind you where the rock rose into a shelter and a windbrake. The whole thing was perfectly designed in Abbie's opinion, right for one, and when she came here she came alone.

She lay down, stretching pleasurably, feeling the warm late sun on her salt-covered limbs. There was no hurry back. Her father and Corinne wouldn't be home until the small hours. Maudie wouldn't worry. She would think Abbie had gone down to St Columb's, maybe stayed for a meal at one of the two hotels as she sometimes did. She could stay here till dark if she liked, and swim back when the stars were in the sky. She liked swimming at night.

She would have to find a bigger rock if she swam out with Bryan, and she closed her eyes and imagined he was here beside her. 'I'm crazy about you,' she heard him say. 'I love you, Abbie.' He always called her Abigail, but no matter. There could be lovely times ahead. They could choose pet names for each other, secret names that no one else knew.

She yawned, snuggling against the smooth warm rock. The builders were coming in to make some alterations to her father's study while he was away filming. A wall was being thrown back for further enlargement. Leo Lansing liked to pace around his study, rehearsing his lines.

38

Abbie would supervise that, and plead, bribe and badger the workmen into completing on schedule, because all must be finished and tidy before the king's return. But she would have time on her hands, lots of time to fall in love.

Her thoughts blurred as she relaxed completely, and she was drowsily following a seagull's flight and thinking it would be nice to be able to fly, when she fell asleep.

Rain on her face woke her, not a light summer drizzle but hard and heavy spots, and she sat up to find that the little clouds had formed a livid thunderous sky and a storm had blown up. She must have been very sound asleep, and there was nothing she could do now but get under the windbrake of rock and wait.

Only in the wildest winters did the sea wash right over this rock. She was in no danger, but she was going to get very cold, and she hoped that the storm would be shortlived.

The wind had turned bitter, and the seas were churning around her, and there wasn't even room enough to trot up and down to keep the circulation going. She had to sit it out.

It was a warning she would remember. She'd known that the weather looked like breaking, and yet she had been fool enough to sleep as peacefully as though she was tucked up in her bed at home.

She sat huddled, her back to the rock, chilled to the bone. She kept her head down, but the rain still reached her; it was a very shallow shelter. Even thinking of Bryan didn't provide enough glow to reduce the goose-pimples or the chattering of her teeth.

She was very glad she had told Maudie she was walking down to the harbour. If she'd said anything about swimming Maudie would have been really concerned by now. Ben hadn't been on the clifftop part of the gardens, so he didn't know where she was either. No

39

one would panic, and she would get back when the storm blew over. A summer storm as fierce and sudden as this was always brief.

Her hair was dripping into her eyes, and she pushed it back and looked out across the swelling sea, to the coastline and her home, and the boats around the harbour, and saw the dinghy, pitching up and down, coming towards her.

It was a white dinghy with a navy or black stripe painted around it, and she recognised it. 'I don't believe it,' she said aloud. And then, 'But it is.'

It was Max Routlege, rowing straight for her rock, and making good headway in spite of the rise and fall. In her white swimsuit she would have been visible from his boat. He must have looked across and seen her, and thought she was in danger, sitting on a small rock, half a mile out, in the middle of a storm.

He thought he was rescuing a swimmer in distress, whereas she was in an awkward position but not in danger. And of course he didn't know who she was. She wondered whether she should pretend that she was at the end of her tether. It was chivalrous of him to come to her rescue—that dinghy didn't look too comfortable, pitching and tossing, and neither did he, although he was wearing oilskins.

He got the dinghy on to the shingle and looked up to where she sat, wiped the rain and sea spray from his eyes, and said, 'Oh no, not you!'

He sounded as though, if he had recognised her before, she could have been washed off the rock before he'd have come to pick her up; as though he was in two minds now whether to row away again. She wasn't keen on a lift back from him anyway. She almost felt she would rather sit out the storm.

'Nobody asked you to come,' she snapped.

'You're a local,' he said. 'You should have seen the storm signs.'

She had had other things on her mind, and then she had fallen asleep. She would have explained about falling asleep, if he hadn't been glaring at her. The rain seemed to be getting worse. At this rate the storm should blow over before long, but she smiled maliciously down into the furious face and said, 'Oh dear, I hope you're not going to get marooned too. There isn't room for both of us.'

'What are you doing out here anyway?' he demanded.

'I was sunbathing.'

'It's quite a swim.'

'It's safe enough if you're a local.'

'Come on.' He took off his oilskins as she slid down the little slope of shingle, and held out an impatient hand. She avoided his hand, but she hadn't realised how chilled and cramped she was, and so stiff so that she couldn't help to shove off the dinghy. She just stood there, shivering, and clambered aboard with an effort.

When he put the oilskin round her she tried to protest through chattering teeth, but he took no notice. The sea itself was calming, the wind dropping, although the rain still fell in torrents, and when the dinghy reached the *Cormorant* Abbie said, 'I would be grateful if you'd take me the rest of the way.'

'I need a drink if you don't,' he said, speaking to her for the first time, attaching the dinghy alongside.

She *was* cold. She probably could swim to the shore, but at the risk of cramp, of her muscles seizing up. A fine gesture of independence it would be to sink to the bottom.

When she stood up she was shivering in the tent of oilskin, and Max Routlege went up the ladder first. He looked back, but this time he didn't hold out a hand and if he had she would have ignored it again. She went slowly up, in her flapping oilskins, clinging tenaciously to the sides of the ladder, almost falling on to the deck; and followed him to the hatchway, shedding her oilskins before she went down into the saloon galley.

Opposite the galley-space two settees faced each other, a table between. Abbie slumped on to one of the settees, closing her eyes, hearing Max Routlege moving around, and murmured automatically, 'Can I do anything?'

'I doubt it,' he said.

Thank *you*, she thought woozily. That's the last offer you get from me. After that she kept her eyes shut until he said, 'Drink this.'

'This' was coffee, laced with rum, in a brown enamel mug. He hadn't asked her if she liked rum. She didn't, but he took no notice of her grimace, and it was warming as she forced it down.

He was drinking whatever he was having in the galley, his back to her, surely a piece of unnecessary boorishness. As she began to feel warmer she began to feel angry.

It was cosier here than it was on the rock, but he hadn't snatched her from a watery grave, so she didn't owe him eternal gratitude. Ever since he'd first set eyes on her yesterday he had been aggressively offensive, going out of his way to insult her. She had no idea why, and now she asked him bluntly, 'Just what do you imagine you've got against me?'

He turned slowly, looking at her over his shoulder with open contempt. 'A few memories,' he said.

'But we've never met before,' she protested.

'Forget it.' He finished his coffee and began to move around the galley.

The boat was well balanced, a stable craft. She could hear the pounding of the rain and see nothing but rain through the portholes, but he seemed entirely occupied with what was going on on the cooking stove.

It looked as though he had been preparing his meal

when he went up on deck—probably to check all was battened down against the storm—and saw the small white figure on the small brown rock across the waves.

The food smelled appetising, and Abbie was beginning to feel hungry, but even if he set a plate in front of her she felt he would begrudge it to her. Probably he'd only cooked for one, and he was capable of eating his supper and ignoring her, even though he had been a guest at her father's table last night.

'A few memories,' he'd said, but he had no memories of Abbie. Maybe they were of somebody who resembled her. Perhaps a pampered rich girl had disappointed him.

She concentrated on her drink, not displeased at that explanation. The girl's name had eluded the gossip writers. There had been no hints of Max Routlege's heart getting a battering. Not his heart, his pride. That was what beat within that brawny chest. Arrogance, pride that some time had taken a fall.

Splendid, thought Abbie. Whoever she was I'd like to shake her hand. She smiled down into her empty mug and Max Routlege said, 'God, you look smug.'

Something about her really rattled him. How close to that other girl did she seem to get? she wondered. 'And why shouldn't you feel smug?' he went on. 'A princess who's never had to do a day's work in her life.' That was all he knew. 'Although take away your father's name,' he said cynically, 'and you're nothing.'

'I don't like you either.' A pang of pure rage got her to her feet, glaring back at him. 'I think you're a boor and probably a bully.' She could never remember speaking like this to anyone before in her whole life, but no one before had ever told her that she counted for nothing. 'I think,' she concluded as a final shot, 'that I'd rather be afloat with a gorilla!'

She ran up the steps to the deck, ran to the boat's edge and dived neatly over. The ten minutes' rest and

43

the warm drink had both helped to revive her, but it was fury that was really fuelling her. She swam straight for her own little cove, and she was sure he would be watching. Although she didn't look back until she felt the sand beneath her feet.

Then she turned towards the *Cormorant*, and was amused to see the dinghy not far behind. He'd *followed* her! He'd thought she was going to get into difficulties again, and that he was responsible this time.

She collected her clothes and clambered up the cliff face, laughing to herself. She had enjoyed the challenge of battling ashore through the tail-end of the storm. She was too exhilarated to feel fatigue, she climbed with swift agility, and when she scrambled on to the cliff top the dinghy was still not quite back at the *Cormorant*.

Whether he could make out her movements or not she waved at him. She'd scared him, or he wouldn't have followed. He thought she was a spoiled little nothing, but she hadn't hung around to be insulted, and that must have surprised him, so there was one opinion he'd have to revise.

Not that Max Routlege's opinions mattered. Her only interest now was getting into the house and getting a hot bath without Maudie discovering what she had been up to. Maudie would have gone on and on, asking how Abbie could have fallen asleep out there and slept till the storm broke.

The answer was that she felt so secure on her little rock. She would have been safe enough, cold but safe. If Max Routlege hadn't come along she would have been thinking of swimming back by now, and no harm done; but she had enjoyed showing him she could look after herself, that she was not quite helpless.

She crept into the house unseen and hurried to her room, and as she closed the door her exhilaration left her. Its aftermath was emptiness. She felt cold and hollow.

Even if she did remind him of some old unlucky affair she wished he hadn't said that about her being nothing. She looked across at her reflection in the dressing table mirror and tried to smile. What had she expected? No face? She had called him a gorilla, a boor and a bully. But none of that could have cut like— you are your father's name and nothing more.

She went into her bathroom and stripped off, rubbing her shoulders and her clammy arms, as she waited for hot water to fill the bath. She was so cold now that she could hardly feel a thing, and from nowhere came the thought——If I remind him of a girl he loved and hated, how did he touch her when he loved her?

CHAPTER THREE

ABBIE plunged into the hot bath, almost scalding her chilled body so that she gasped and jumped up again, lowering herself very gingerly this time. She was still tense when she was warm and comfortable and should have been relaxed, and she lay in the scented water, scolding herself.

Why was she wondering about Max Routlege as a lover? What a revolting, incongruous thought! She should be thinking about Bryan. She had to think about Bryan as much as possible in the next two days. Bryan was crazy about her, and that meant she was more than her father's shadow. If she married Bryan she would have another name, although she would keep Lansing.

She was proud to be a Lansing, and how could she let Max Routlege dominate her mind so that she kept remembering what he had said, and hating him for it? She had never hated anyone, but no one had touched her raw nerves as he did, blaming her for memories in which she had no part.

She would keep away from Max Routlege like the plague in future, and although she couldn't honestly tell Bryan that she loved him she could admit that she found him attractive, and she liked having him near.

Bryan was as nice as a warm bath after swimming in a stormy sea, and she towelled herself dry and dressed and went down to Maudie in the kitchen, glowing.

Maudie rounded on her accusingly. 'I never heard you come in. Why didn't you tell me you were back? I've been worried about you.'

'I got caught in the storm,' said Abbie meekly. 'I went straight up to change.'

'Where were you?' Maudie wanted to know, and she would probably find out. Max Routlege would probably tell someone, and it would get around, so Abbie admitted,

'In Max Routlege's boat.' She'd leave the details of how she got there for somebody else to fill in.

'Him who came to dinner last night?'

'The same.'

'Ooh!' Abbie could follow Maudie's train of thought by her expression before Maudie asked, 'You like him, do you?'

'Not particularly,' said Abbie, which was the understatement of the year.

Talking about Max Routlege brought back the contempt in his eyes, and his wounding words, and drained away the warmth as though her blood was running thin. So she talked about everything else, and there was plenty to talk about with Maudie.

But when she went to bed she couldn't sleep. She heard the car when her father and Corinne came home. Publicity said they were having an affair. Leo Lansing's name was often linked with his current leading lady, but no one expected him to marry again. Everyone knew that Helen had been the great love of his life, and that now the woman for whom he cared most was his daughter.

More than one of his girl-friends had blamed Abbie for 'turning Leo against them', although Abbie had never done any such thing. She would have been happy if he had remarried, she only wanted his happiness. She believed it was the memory of her mother that kept him from a second marriage. In fact, it was selfishness ...

In Abbie's dreams she was swimming again, fighting the sea. It was harder in the dream than it had been in reality, and she woke tossing, the bedclothes on the floor. She was glad to wake. There had been no sign of the shore in her dream, nothing to make for. She had been swimming blind, wasting her strength and getting nowhere.

Corinne left soon after breakfast, kissing Abbie and thanking her for everything and hoping they would meet again soon. Maybe they would. Abbie might go out to where they were on location. Sometimes her father asked her to. If magazines were interviewing him he sometimes liked Abbie to be in the picture.

Tomorrow Leo would be on his way too. Today Abbie had his packing to finish, his little medical case of pills and potions to fill up. There were all sorts of things for Abbie to attend to while Leo rested today, relaxing indoors.

They ate dinner together, Leo reading his script and the newspapers. Sometimes he quite forgot Abbie was there. Like all the best servicing devices she performed quietly, without a hitch. But tonight, as he ate his dinner, he noticed Maudie.

'Maudie's slowing down,' he announced, and Abbie said quickly,

'She still runs this house like clockwork. We'd never find another Maudie.'

Leo grunted at that and dismissed Maudie from his thoughts, but there was something else before he went. 'This young man of yours,' he said, 'what's his name? Bryan Gibson.' Last night Leo had seen Bryan laying a slight claim to Abbie, and he had no intention of letting that develop in his absence. 'Is he likely to get serious?' he asked his daughter now, the laughter lines creasing around his eyes, his mouth drawn into a humorous line so that Abbie smiled.

'I don't know.'

Until Bryan told her in so many words that he loved her she hadn't the confidence to claim that he did.

'He seems a nice enough chap.' Leo sounded anxious

to be fair. 'But he'll never rate much, too anxious to please. I want a real man for you,' said Leo. 'Not a yes-man.'

'Yes, of course,' said Abbie, 'so do I. But I've got such a marvellous father that it's hard to find anyone who measures up to him.'

Leo beamed at her. He couldn't have agreed more.

Next morning he drove away with his agent, a neat precise man, who would be staying around the filming area for the first few weeks to make sure his star client was happy in his work.

Abbie waved them both goodbye. Right from when she was a little girl the house had always seemed empty when her father left. But this time there were the builders to deal with, that would provide some occupation for her, and of course there was Bryan.

She went into the study to file and tidy, and Maudie brought in a lunch tray of coffee and sandwiches and said, 'You'll be out this evening?'

'Yes, I'm going to this party.'

Maudie looked disapprovingly at the papers on the desk. Abbie was making up the latest scrapbook of her father's cuttings and Maudie would have preferred to see her getting on with her own life. She said, 'You ought to be thinking about a holiday.'

'I don't need a holiday,' Abbie teased her. 'My life's one long——'

'With some friends of your own,' said Maudie. It was true that when Abbie visited it was always her father's friends. But now there was Bryan, and she smiled.

'And I'll be going to the party tonight with a very nice young man.'

'The one with the boat?' Maudie sounded quite eager, and when Abbie said,

'No,' she sighed. 'With Bryan,' said Abbie. 'It's Bryan I'm going around with these days. You know that.' Maudie had seen Bryan collecting Abbie, and

Abbie had returned from her dates with him and told Maudie where they had been and what they'd done.

Last night as Maudie served the meal she had had her first glimpse of Max Routlege. The glimpse had been cursory, the character assessment a snap judgment, but when Abbie came back after the storm on Saturday and said she had been on Max Routlege's boat Maudie had been pleased. Unless she was much mistaken there was a man who would be a match for Leo. If Abbie got a man like that Leo could look out. But with Bryan it was going to be the same old story.

'Oh, *him*,' sniffed Maudie, and stomped off, banging the door behind her.

Abbie smiled a little. If Bryan did ask her to marry him, and if she seriously considered it, then perhaps Maudie would explain why she had said, 'Oh, *him*,' and why she seemed to prefer Max Routlege. It could be because she was following the Max Routlege TV series and enjoying them, whereas she'd heard nothing exciting about Bryan. It could be that Max Routlege had thanked her when she put dinner plates in front of him on Friday night, and Bryan hadn't. Maudie always had her reasons, but in this case she knew neither man.

If she had heard half that Max Routlege had said to Abbie she would have been ready to scratch his eyes out, while Bryan cared for Abbie and showed it in tender cherishing ways. And tonight he had something very serious to say to her.

She had met quite a number of Bryan's friends these last few weeks, but tonight's would be her first visit to the party house, her first meeting with her hosts, and when she had asked what she should wear, Bryan had said, 'You'll look beautiful any way.'

'Thank you,' she said. 'But is it casual wear or party gear?'

'Dress up,' said Bryan. 'I've told them a princess is coming.'

'I hope you haven't.' He was joking, of course. He'd laughed and she'd joined in, but it did mean that he wanted her in her finery, wearing some of the famous jewellery her father had bought her.

She spent a long time that evening going through her wardrobe, because it wasn't just a dress for a party she was selecting. It could be the dress she wore when Bryan asked her to marry him, so it had to be special. At last she chose a dress of white-and-silver elegance, and twined a string of perfectly matched pearls around her throat. Her make-up was cool and pearl-like and her hair was smooth. This was how she always looked. Not on the rock, of course, in the middle of the storm, nor on Max Routlege's boat, but this was Abigail Lansing and she had to keep Max Routlege out of her mind if she didn't want to spend the evening scowling.

That was what she was doing now, glaring into the mirror, so she made herself smile instead.

Bryan would be arriving any time, and she was a little nervous. She went across to the window with its calming panorama of sea and sky. There were birds in the sky but no planes. Her father would have flown to France by now. He would be meeting old and new colleagues. She could picture the scene and she wished she could have been part of it. The film would be a great success, she knew it would.

She couldn't see the *Cormorant* out there on the sealine, and she wondered if it had really sailed away this time or if it would be back again later tonight, and gave herself an impatient little shake. The boat had gone, so had Max Routlege, and yet she was still letting her thoughts dwell on him.

This was Bryan's evening. Perhaps she should keep saying Bryan-Bryan-Bryan, silently like a mantra, and now she would go downstairs and wait for Bryan. She would open the hall door so that she could see his car coming down the driveway, and hurry to meet him.

She would run, smiling, hands outstretched, and he would jump out of the car and catch her hands, and draw her towards him. And kiss her differently perhaps, because from tonight things would be different between them.

In the hall the freesias that Bryan had brought her were drooping, although she had changed the water each day. Their fragrance was fading, she had to bury her face in them to catch any hint of it.

She opened the hall door and stood framed in the doorway, but when the car came she didn't run. She went across the terrace and down the three shallow circular steps, but not running and not with outstretched hands. Something held her back. Some part of her suddenly wanted to delay the moment of decision when she would have to commit herself to loving Bryan.

When he asked her to marry him it would be all right, but she didn't want him to ask her for a little while. It would be better to get the party over first.

If he asked her before they got to the party then there would be people milling around, Bryan's friends, Bryan telling them maybe, but this had to be private, without an audience. On the way home. That would be best.

She realised that she was breathing shallowly, her mind in a state of flurry, and she clasped her hands tighter together and kept a steady smile on her face. 'You're more fantastic every time I see you,' said Bryan, getting out of the car and looking at her as though he couldn't believe his eyes. 'There won't be another girl tonight to hold a candle to you.'

It was unlikely there would be another girl wearing a string of pearls like Abigail's. But take away the pearls, she thought wryly, and I'm unlikely to light up any room. Still, it was nice to be told she was fantastic. Bryan's admiration was very cheering and she got into the car beside him, thinking how lovely it was to be with someone who was crazy about her.

Bryan didn't talk seriously on their way to the party, he talked brightly. About the people she would be meeting tonight, about his day, about her father and the film he would be starting on tomorrow.

'I've always fancied getting into the film business,' said Bryan. 'Behind the cameras, of course.' And they discussed examples of superb photography in films her father had starred in. Abbie knew every shot in those. When Leo gave private movie shows for his guests at Players' Court the films were usually his own.

The party was in a large modern flat, already over-flowing when they arrived, but Bryan shoved his way through and almost everybody seemed to know him. The couple giving the party were young and beautiful, and when Bryan said, 'This is Abigail Lansing,' they both said, 'Of course,' as though they had been waiting for her.

'I fell in love with your father when I was six years old,' the girl said rapturously, 'and I'm still in love with him.'

It was like the other parties Abbie had been to. This was why people asked her, because she brought a little of her father's glamour with her. She didn't mind. She answered the professional questions about his career, and personal things about him as a man and a wonderful father. No one ever asked Abbie her opinion about anything, but they were fascinated by her father's views, and she was his loving mouthpiece.

When one conversation ended she looked around for Bryan. He had been with her most of the evening and she certainly wasn't checking on him. She just looked for him, and drifted around, with a drink in her hand, vaguely seeking him.

She had almost rounded a corner when she heard a man say, 'You're a lucky devil,' and Bryan's voice, confidential and slightly slurred with alcohol,

'She's a frigid fish, but you can't have everything, and it can't hurt to be seen around with King Leo's daughter.'

The other man's laughter was knowing and Abbie drew back, thankful that she could. It would have been horrible if she had been one step further and walked round the corner as Bryan spoke.

She turned, still holding her drink in a steady hand, realising that no one else had overheard. The whole thing had been hardly louder than a whisper, the two men must have had their heads together, but recognising Bryan's voice had sharpened her hearing. She went back to where the guests were thickest, clustered around the bar, and in no time someone else was talking to her about her father.

Soon Bryan came seeking her. Abbie smiled when he put a hand on her shoulder, evading his touch although she was determined to get home before she let herself feel anything. She played her part for the best part of another hour and then said, 'I want to go home.'

Bryan's jaw sagged. The party was swinging and would be till morning from the looks of it. 'Aren't you enjoying yourself?' he asked.

She ran fingertips between her eyes. 'I've got a headache.' She wasn't quite lying. Later she would have a headache and a heartache, although right now she was holding the aches at bay. She said quietly, 'I don't want to drag you away, if you'd get me a taxi.'

She had considered phoning for a taxi herself, but that would have caused all sorts of fuss. And Bryan wasn't going to call a taxi and send King Leo's daughter home alone. She had no choice but to leave with him and go on acting a little longer.

'Of course I'll take you home,' he was saying now.

After tonight she wasn't sure how she would handle

the situation. She couldn't see him again, but she couldn't tell anyone why. Maybe she'd take Maudie's advice and have a holiday, and come back even more of a frigid fish so far as Bryan Gibson was concerned. The relationship, that had never been a relationship, could die a natural death and Bryan could explain that, as best he could, to himself and his friends.

He had an arm around her now and was offering her excuse of a headache to their hosts, and the others who were asking why they were leaving. Abbie went to a commiserating chorus, and faces that seemed sympathetic while she could see them, but she was sure showed very different expressions as soon as she passed by.

Their hosts came to the car with them, the girl still proffering headache pills. 'Are you sure you won't have one? They're awfully good.'

'No, thank you,' said Abbie. 'I get these headaches, and the only cure is to get some sleep. It was a lovely party, I had a lovely time, thank you very much.'

'See you again soon?' said the girl.

'Oh yes,' said Abbie.

She wondered if she should insist on driving, but Bryan was showing no signs now of having drunk too much, and she might have imagined the slurring of his speech when he was discussing her. He seemed sober enough, so that was his sober opinion, and goodness knows how often he'd given it before, how many had been told that she was a cold fish but a gilt-edged status symbol for an up-and-coming young man.

Bryan did most of the talking on their way back to Players' Court and Abbie put in the occasional murmured word. They sounded much as they had on their way out, except that Bryan asked from time to time how her head was and fussed about getting cool air on her face.

They even got back to her father's films and Bryan

said again, 'I'd like to get into film production myself.'
He gave her a sideways glance. 'How about putting in a
word for me with your father some time?'

But of course, this was the serious matter he wanted
to discuss with her. What could be more serious than
Bryan's future and Abbie's influence on his behalf?
Except that she had no influence, and her father would
never in the world promote a lightweight like Bryan
Gibson. That stopped it being serious so that she
wanted to laugh and she felt sick, both together. She
said, 'You're an ambitious young man.'

'I've got plans,' said Bryan, smiling, and she smiled
too because he wasn't worth fighting. She didn't even
say, 'Don't include me in any of your plans,' although
she and Bryan were through. It was over, hopeless, useless.

They stopped to open the gates of Players' Court,
and then finally in the driveway where Abbie
opened her car door before Bryan could, and said as she stepped out, 'Go back to your party.'

'Not without you.' He sounded shocked at the suggestion. 'What are you going to do?'

He expected to be asked into the house. When she
closed the car door he wound down the window, leaning out.

'I've got a headache,' she reminded him. 'I'm going
to bed.'

'Poor Abigail,' he said tenderly.

You can say that again, she thought. 'Goodnight,'
she said, and went before he could get out of the car
and try to kiss her goodnight, which he might have
done even though he considered her a cold fish.

Maudie would be in bed, but even Maudie would
have been unwelcome tonight. Abbie went upstairs to
her room through the quiet darkened house, glad
there were no guests and that her father had gone. She
needed to be alone and until she closed her bedroom

door she didn't really know what was going to happen to her.

She might cry till morning, she might cower shivering in a chair all night. She might go completely to pieces. She had held herself on such a tight rein of restraint since she overheard Bryan that she had no clear idea what her reaction would be when she did give way.

She closed the door behind her, and a hot burning blush scalded her face to the hairline as though she was hearing Bryan's words for the first time, and dry sobs shook her. Oh, it hurt. It was such a humiliating betrayal because he had acted as though he cared for her and she had needed someone to care.

After what Max Routlege said she had *needed* Bryan. She hadn't fallen in love with him, thank God, not as near as she had come to loving Stephen. But she was desperately lonely now because she had believed Bryan was a friend, and he had never even been that. No one had. She had no friends of her own. In all the world only Max and Ben, and Miss Lupton who had been her governess and who still kept in touch, thought she was of real worth.

She didn't realise that she hadn't included her father in the list.

She walked blindly across to the window. Her eyes were burning like her face, and she needed air.

There were navigation lights out there, the *Cormorant*'s could be among them, and she said aloud, 'Are you sleeping soundly, Max Routlege? You would have enjoyed tonight. Of course I've known for years that I was nothing but my father's daughter, but tonight I had it spelled out for me again. Not face to face as you told me, but the way people usually say these kind of things, when they don't think you're listening.'

She had always known in her heart, it was the crux

57

of her insecurity, but the only man who had ever been honest with her was Max Routlege. He had said what everyone thought, and hid behind compliments and kisses. He believed she had never done a day's work in her life and he despised her for being a hanger-on. The rest pretended to admire her for it.

Max Routlege was right. She was nothing but her father's name, with looks that were a plain edition of her mother's. She had never been herself, never Abbie. Always Abigail Lansing, King Leo's daughter.

She didn't even know what she ought to look like. That whole wardrobe of clothes could have been theatrical costumes to suit the part she played. Even the make-up she wore was pale like Helen's, and the smooth way she dressed her hair was copied from pictures of her mother.

'You're never going to be beautiful,' her father had said, 'but so long as you wear beautiful clothes they'll never find out.'

But they had found out. Everyone knew why she looked beautiful. 'More fantastic every time I see you,' Bryan had said. 'Dress up,' he had told her, 'they're expecting a princess.' So she had put on the pearls and he had joked with his friends that she was a frigid fish but it couldn't hurt to be seen around with her father's daughter.

She unclasped the pearls and dropped them on the dressing table. Then she got out of the dress and returned it to the wardrobe, and suddenly straightened her shoulders as though she was shaking off a heavier garment than the dress had been, and turned from the wardrobe tossing back her hair.

None of them knew the first thing about her. She was not frigid. She worked, and she would have welcomed a chance to work harder. Abigail Lansing might seem as pampered and useless as Max Routlege had said, but nobody had ever got close enough to meet Abbie.

She had let Bryan gently off the hook tonight. If she had turned on him at the party she could have made him a laughing stock. Or sparing him that she could at least have told him a few home truths before she said goodbye for the last time.

But Bryan wasn't worth bothering with. He was an opportunist whose good opinion could be bought any day. Now Max Routlege was a very different matter. If she could ever get him to eat his words it would soothe her bruised ego more than a hundred Bryans bringing her freesias and pretending she was beautiful.

And there just might be a way to do that. She had a few weeks before her father would be wanting to see her. A few weeks of freedom ahead, although she had never thought of being apart from her father as freedom before.

She took off her make-up. She would never be anywhere near as lovely as her mother. In her present mood her mouth was so pugnacious that she looked more like a peasant in revolt than a princess, and she was surprised to hear herself giggle.

It wasn't hysterics either. Of course she was hurt. She had just been jilted again, in a nastier fashion than any of the others, but it wasn't going to destroy her. She was going to fight back.

Max Routlege was the challenge. If she could show him she was not a non-person, she was tough enough and strong enough when she needed to be, then she could face them all and laugh at this nonsense of her being 'King Leo's princess'.

Of course she would be here when her father needed her. He was the most wonderful man in the world and she hero-worshipped him with an unquestioning devotion. She believed that he would understand, and she

59

slept soundly and woke with a feeling of excitement.

She went to the window, and *Cormorant* was out there, so a little luck was on her side. She dressed in jeans, a white-towelling T-shirt and a pair of rope sandals, and packed a draw-top bag with a few more serviceable clothes. Then she took her pearls downstairs and put them in the wall safe.

There were several flat jewellery cases in there, and there wasn't a thing she had chosen herself. Her father bought what he chose. It was all Abigail, and Abbie closed the safe and replaced the painting.

Passing through the hall she saw that the freesias were dead. She carried them into the kitchen to the rubbish bin, closing the lid with a little sigh. They had been lovely. Their perfume had been sweet.

She was down before Maudie this morning, and before Ben and Audrey had arrived. She had the breakfast cooking and the kettle boiling when Maudie came into the kitchen, and as soon as Maudie was settled with a cup of tea Abbie said, 'That holiday you were saying I should take, I'm going to. On a boat. I'll find someone to take me aboard.'

There were plenty of luxury boats around the Cornish coast at this time of year. Some of them were owned by her father's sailing friends, who visited Players' Court, and would certainly give Abigail Lansing a holiday afloat if she wanted one.

But she was aiming for the *Cormorant*. No other boat would serve her purpose, and when Maudie said, 'What about Mr Routlege? They say he's got a very nice boat,' Abbie tried to sound casual.

'Yes, he has. Yes, I might try him.'

As soon as everything was settled with Maudie she went down to the harbour, carrying her kit bag. Apart from a few holidaymakers, sitting on the two benches and the sea wall, reading the newspapers they had just bought from the newsagents, the only folk around the harbour this early were the boating fraternity and local fishermen.

The ones who knew Abbie saw something different about her this morning. She wasn't usually dressed so casually, and her hair was tied back in a swathe from which tendrils escaped. Without her discreet and impeccable make-up she looked younger. None of them pinned it down, but exchanging good mornings they sensed a change somewhere.

She borrowed an inflatable dinghy, from a couple she knew who were just coming in from their small motor cruiser, and paddled out to the *Cormorant*. Twice she had watched Max Routlege rowing towards her. This time he was watching her. She wondered if she was recognised, dressed this way, fairish hair held back with a thin brown ribbon. Lots of girls looked like this.

He was leaning over the deck rail when she drew alongside. 'Mistress of disguises, aren't you?' he said. 'What is it today?'

'Good morning.' She smiled up, but he didn't smile down. She held the boat stationary, blocking the current with her paddle, and decided on the direct approach. 'That offer you made to take me on as a deckhand. If it's still open, I'll take it.'

His eyebrows rose. 'I thought you'd rather be afloat with a gorilla.'

She'd expected this, and an apology was due to him. What he had said to her had seemed to be the truth. What she had said had been sheer abuse. Well, most of it. He might be a boor and a bully, but he was probably preferable to a gorilla. She said meekly, 'I'm sorry about that. That wasn't polite, especially after you'd given me a lift half way home, and a hot drink.'

It was very important for her to make him admit he was wrong about her. That was all she needed, one word of acceptance from a man who was no hypocrite.

61

She asked, 'Where are you sailing?'

'Round the coast.'

'You could throw me off, then, if I didn't work my passage.'

'*You?* Work your passage?'

'*Yes.*' Her voice was clear and carrying, and his expression became a shade less derisive.

'Why should you want to come sailing with me?' he demanded. He knew she wasn't attracted to him. 'Is the local press after another paragraph, or have you had a row with your boy-friend?'

She winced when he spoke of her boy-friend and said shrilly, 'I just need a change of scene. There's no one at home right now and I like sailing.' She was wondering if he had noticed that pang of near pain when he said abruptly,

'Right, princess, you're on.'

She had never thought it could be this easy. His sudden capitulation astonished her and she sounded astonished. 'You'll take me?'

He grinned, laughing at her. 'What kind of an offer is that?'

'I'm sure I'll be safe enough,' she said wryly.

'Oh, you will.' Such an emphatic denial of any designs on her was uncomplimentary, but she knew how he felt about her. The way she felt about him. That she wouldn't want him if he was the last member of the opposite sex breathing. She wasn't foolhardy enough to get herself alone on a boat with a man who might turn unwelcomely amorous. She'd need no chaperone on the *Cormorant*.

'So when do we sail?' she asked.

'With the tide. Take that back.' He meant the skiff. 'I'll follow and pick you up.' He put the light aluminium ladder over the side, hooking it on to the deck rail, came down it and reached for her bag, asking, 'You were sure of yourself, weren't you? The lady wants, the lady gets. Hasn't anyone ever said no to you?'

'Yes.' The men she had thought might be falling in love with her had all said no by going away. She had been refused before, as she had been by Bryan last night, and she was scared now that Max Routlege was about to go back on his offer. But he took her bag and went with it down the hatchway.

She returned the skiff to its spot on the beach, took off her rope sandals and waded out to meet Max and clambered aboard his dinghy. They didn't do much talking. Abbie said the weather looked promising, the storm didn't seem to have broken the fine spell. Max replied in grunts, so she shut up. She didn't want to irritate him.

It had been raining so hard on her last visit that she hadn't taken much notice of the general layout, but she looked around now, following him down a companionway, and down three steps into a two-berth cabin. The berths ran either side, with a dressing-table-cum-locker between, and he said, 'Here you are,' opening a door on a washbasin and toilet facilities.

'But this is luxury!' she said.

'Comparative luxury.' His voice made her turn and stare. For some reason he was amused, and it was not kindly humour. This man didn't like her. He was taking her along, but he didn't like her, and she was conscious of a quickening of her pulse that was almost fear.

Not that there could be anything to be afraid of. If she found she couldn't stand a confined space with Max Routlege she could always get off the boat again; he was only sailing round the coastline.

'Can you handle a boat?' he was asking her.

'I've been sailing with friends, I've taken the wheel sometimes. I will work my passage, I can cook and clean.'

'Done much of that, have you?' he said sardonically, and she said very softly,

'You would be surprised.'

This time he didn't say that she couldn't surprise him. Perhaps he was remembering when he did say that, to Abbie dressed like a princess, flowers in her hands, Bryan in what seemed to be adoring attendance, and contrasting her with the girl who stood here now.

'Have you had breakfast?' she asked.

'Yes.'

'What do you do about meals?'

'Take my main meal at night and a cold snack for lunch.'

'Have you fixed tonight's or can I?'

'The galley's all yours,' he said. 'This way.'

The cooker and sink stretched the full length of the saloon, and when Max left her she opened the drawers and the lockers, finding pans and cutlery and an adequate stock of food.

All her other boat trips had been with upward of half a dozen others aboard. This was almost as good as being alone, because she knew that Max Routlege wouldn't seek her company. She supposed he was taking her along to watch her make a fool of herself, and she was fiercely determined that he should see no such thing.

When she heard the anchors being hauled aboard she went up on deck and stayed aft as the boat drew away from St Columb's Cove, watching the coastline and the three snowy billowing sails. Salt spray rose from the sea, and the craziness of what she was doing was splendidly exhilarating.

This was escape. It might not seem so much, hitching a boat trip with a man who knew her father and didn't fancy her anyway. She wasn't risking much in that set-up. But she felt quite idiotically reckless and different, so very different.

There would be no more men like Bryan, who made much of her only because her name was Abigail Lansing. She was no princess. She was Abbie, reborn in the salt spray. From today she would be reckoned with as Abbie.

She could see Max Routlege at the wheel in the centre cockpit. Head and broad shoulders. She didn't want him to find her attractive, she didn't want him to like her. All she wanted was for him to admit he had misjudged her, and before long he would.

Not in words maybe, he seemed a stubborn character, but he'd change his mind about her when he'd tasted her cooking. That made her smile, the idea of her cooking her way into Max Routlege's approval, and at that moment he came along the sloping skid-proofed deck towards her.

She waited for him to speak, but he didn't. He went astern to the self-steering device fixed to the rudder, and then he went below deck with hardly a passing glance at her. That was the pattern of the next two hours. In a thirty-three-foot boat it wasn't easy to keep permanently out of sight and sound of each other, but he managed to ignore her most of the time.

He was probably regretting letting her aboard. There was no land in sight now and it might be unwise to ask him which was their next port of call, in case he said he was dropping her there. When he came up on deck again she went down to the galley, and made coffee and brought his up.

He thanked her and she didn't hang around. It was enough to be surging on over the deep bright water, she didn't care where they were going. She made up her bunk with a sleeping bag, a pillow and a blanket she found in a locker beneath the bunk; and hung the few clothes she had brought with her in the hanging wardrobe.

She checked on the ingredients available, decided

on corned beef sandwiches for the midday snack, and a casserole for the evening meal. About four o'clock she would prepare the casserole and put it to cook slowly in the galley stove. They would obviously eat the evening meal together, facing each other across the little teak table, and she would say something like, 'Do you think you could forget that I'm Abigail Lansing? It isn't my fault that everyone's heard of my father.'

She didn't look like Abigail Lansing, dressed like this, with no make-up on her shining face, pottering around with pots and pans, and dodging Max Routlege as though they were playing hide and seek.

I must be a masochist, she told herself cheerfully, offering my services to him free gratis and for nothing. If I had to prove I'm one of the world's workers I could surely have found a more congenial way of doing it.

But she was enjoying herself, and when she glanced through a saloon porthole and saw land she went up for a better look. There had been nothing but sea to see a few minutes before, and now there was an island on the skyline, rising out of the mists, and they were heading for it. A saddleback island with a peak at either end, about a mile and a half long, she reckoned, with birds filling the skies above and floating on the water around.

Max was back at the wheel now, taking the boat between sharp white pointed rocks that looked like giant teeth, into a deep-water cove with no beach at all, where the sea lapped against the cliffs.

When the throb of the engines died away and the anchors were going down she asked, 'Where are we?'

'I'm home,' he said.

He lowered the ladder to the dinghy and carried down a large cardboard box. As he came up the ladder she asked, 'You've got a home here?'

'Yes.'

The island looked deserted. She couldn't see anything remotely like a house. He went towards the hatchway and she followed him, calling after him as he disappeared down the steps, 'Where is this home of yours?'

'The other side of the island.'

'Do you have any neighbours?'

'If you mean humans, no.'

She pondered on that until he reappeared, carrying another box, then she asked, 'How long are we staying here?'

'I'm staying a fortnight.' He went past her across the deck to the ladder. 'I don't know about you.'

She gasped and swallowed, shocked speechless. He had said he was sailing around the coast, not a word about being marooned on an uninhabited island. She felt cheated and furiously angry, and finding her voice shrieked at him, 'I am not sitting it out here for a fortnight!'

'Please yourself.' He pointed ahead, across the sea. 'That way it's just over thirty miles back to Cornwall.' He turned towards the right and pointed again. 'Or that way it's nearer seventy to the Scillies. However you go there's a hell of a swim ahead of you.'

CHAPTER FOUR

'Is this supposed to be a joke?' Abbie asked icily.

'More in the nature of an experiment,' said Max.

'Would you mind explaining that?' It sounded sinister. He carried the box down into the dinghy and she leaned over the top of the ladder, demanding shrilly, 'What are you planning to do? Dissect me?'

'After a fashion.' As he came up the ladder she stepped back. On deck he stood looking at her from beneath hooded lids, and it gave her the shudders. 'I'm a writer,' he said, as though this was new information to her. His voice was pleasant enough, except for a hint of something held in check as he went on, 'People interest me. You interest me. I'll be interested to see how a girl like you stands up to the rugged life.'

Two weeks with him on a deserted island might get very rugged indeed, and she didn't think he was looking at her so much as at that other girl he'd thought was like her. Perhaps she was simply 'copy' to him, a character to be filed for a future book, but she suspected that he wanted to see her shattered as a stand-in for some pampered girl who had jilted him. 'You must be out of your mind,' she said, and he grinned slowly.

'If I am you're in bad trouble.'

Of course he wasn't, but she hadn't bargained for this. Life wasn't rugged aboard the boat. Below deck was warm and snug and cosy. 'This is luxury,' she had said when he'd shown her what she'd thought was her cabin.

'Comparative luxury,' he'd replied. Compared with what? With his home on the other side of the island?

'We come back here to sleep, I suppose?' she said.

'No.'

'You mean that once off this boat I'm on that island for a fortnight?'

'Yes.'

'Yes, nothing. I'm staying right here.' She folded her arms and took a firm stance. He could hardly throw her into the dinghy. She got the slow grin again and he shook his head.

'To clear off as soon as my back's turned? No chance. You're coming where I can keep an eye on you.' He was a big man, and he was telling her that she was his prisoner. 'You wanted a change of scene,' he said. 'Have you been here before?'

'No.' Her denial sounded strangled.

'Then look around,' drawled Max Routlege. 'There's plenty to see. Are you interested in flora and fauna? Apart from hothouse plants and caged birds.'

Caged birds? She had never caged anything in her life, unless she counted herself. She was about to tell him he was a lousy character judge when his hard fingers closed on her bare arm, drawing her towards the ladder top. The implacable force of his grip unlocked something primitive and wild in her and she screamed and twisted, hitting out at his bare chest with clenched and flying fists. He held her still, but he held her away. 'Don't get hysterical, princess,' he said.

He was clamping her arms to her sides so that she was helpless. She couldn't reach him by kicking, she tried, and then she said, 'I am not hysterical.'

Abigail Lansing had never fought with anyone, not even verbally, much less physically. So much for the new Abbie who now tried belatedly for a little dignity, saying coldly, 'I'm not afraid of you, don't think it. Just get your hands off me.'

He did but, without touching her, his strong hands guided her. As she drew away from him she reached the side of the boat and climbed over the side and went down the ladder, and sat stiffly upright, facing him.

As he pushed the dinghy away from the *Cormorant* she ignored him, and surveyed the scenery as though she was on a culture tour, with cool curiosity. She would have given a lot for the chance to relive the past five minutes and change them. She was furious with herself, clawing at Max Routlege like an alley cat, but when he caught hold of her she had felt as though a hammer had been thrown at her, and her instinctive reaction had been violent.

The air rose cool from the sea, and as the angry colour faded from her cheeks the tension began to leave her too, and she began to see the things she was looking at. They hadn't gone right into the cove, where the water lapped the cliff face. They were rounding the peak, and high up, overlooking the sea, hundreds of birds seemed to be nesting.

Max hadn't said a word, but she had to ask, 'If you're the only one here have you bought the island?'

'Yes.'

'When?'

'A few weeks ago.'

'Then you weren't looking for a house around Pen-rann?'

'I was, until I found this.'

He had kept this quiet, and she could understand why. The longer she looked at it the more she liked the thought of a whole secret island to explore. She couldn't understand why she had panicked just now.

The house might be rugged, but she'd wanted an exercise in survival to prove herself to herself. Max Routlege had done her a favour, bringing her here. She said, 'It makes my rock seem very small.'

'Your rock?' He didn't know what she was talking about, he didn't know anything about her.

She trailed her hand in the water, a pretty pale ringless hand with long nails manicured in oyster pink. 'The rock I swim out to,' she said.

He knew that one, where he had wasted time and energy 'saving' her from the storm, although in retrospect she was glad he had turned up. She had been cold, and would have been colder and cramped before the storm blew over. It was possible she wouldn't have managed to swim back, or even to reach the boats. It was possible he had saved her life, and she frowned, considering that, because she didn't want to be grateful to him.

'Why do you call it yours?' he was asking her.

'Because when I'm there no one can reach me.' Then she had to smile, 'Yes, I know there's a first time for everything,' and she had to go on, 'Thank you, I've just been realising I might not have made it back.'

'I think you would.' They were round the peak, coming down the coastline of the plain. 'You're a strong swimmer,' he said.

'But not strong enough to swim back to Cornwall.' She looked at the birds, squinting, a hand shielding her eyes from the sun. She spotted, 'A razorbill, and a puffin. Is this a bird sanctuary?'

'Yes. The cottage was used when preservationists called here, but last winter's gales stripped off most of the roof.' She followed his gaze and saw the cottage, built of grey stone and well back from the beach. From here it wasn't easy to see if anyone had put back the tiles, and there was no point in asking, she'd know soon enough.

Then she saw the seals gambolling on the beach and squealed in delight, 'Seals!' She was out of the boat as he beached it, watching them flippering their way back into the sea, where the smooth round heads bobbed about at a safe distance, and seemed to be keeping an eye on the proceedings.

71

Max was almost at the cottage, and she picked up the box he had left, the smaller one although it was heavy enough, and followed over the sand and the shingle. It was rocky where the cottage stood, and there was sparse tough grass here and there.

The roof looked as though it was being professionally repaired ; the slatting was completed, although there was still a section of tiles unhung. Tiles and ladders were stacked in front of the house.

The door was open. Max had gone inside and she followed him, putting down her box on an ugly old table. There was a chair, a dark-brown painted cupboard reaching from floor to ceiling, and a small range that was dull and beginning to rust.

'It's rugged,' she said. 'Not counting the hole in the roof.'

'That should be fixed by tonight.' It was coming up to midday, there was plenty of daylight ahead. She asked,

'Are you doing it?'

He opened the box he had carried, which was full of food and tins and packages. As he began to transfer the contents of the box to the cupboard shelves he said, 'Yes.'

'You've made a good job of it so far.'

'Thank you.' She ignored the irony in that.

'So let's get on with it,' she said, 'because I bet I'll be sleeping under the hole in the roof.'

When he laughed this time it sounded different, although he asked, 'Are you up to hard labour, princess?'

'I'll make a bargain with you.' She handed him two cans of tomato soup from the box and he put them on the top shelf. 'I've never tiled a roof before, but if you'll stop calling me princess, and tell me what you want me to do, I'll work as hard as you and as long.'

He hadn't expected this. She was suddenly sure that

the girl of whom she reminded him wouldn't have said it in a hundred years, and that cheered her so that she smiled and added, 'It isn't generally known, but I'm as strong as an ox.'

He raised a quizzical eyebrow and agreed, 'No, it isn't generally known.' It was hard to tell what he was thinking. 'No princess?' he said. 'Just Abigail?'

'Abbie.'

'All right, Abbie. Will you finish stacking this stuff away?'

'Yes, of course,' she said. He went outside, and through the window she watched him lifting and fixing the ladder, then she got on with emptying the two cardboard boxes. The top shelf of the cupboard was going to be a stretch for her, so she put the rest on the lower shelves and in some sort of order. There was enough food here for several days, and other supplies still on the boat. Their diet need not be too spartan.

She opened a door into a smaller room where there was a stone sink but no taps, and a bucket under the take-away pipe. A five-gallon plastic container probably held fresh water, and on shelves over the sink were a couple of saucepans, a frying pan, a kettle and a little camping Calor gas cooker.

There were also several large tins of paint around and sacks of something that was probably cement, and at the back of the cottage she saw piles of timber. The material was all here for the house renovation, all that was needed was the workers, and here she was, part of the labour force.

Upstairs there were two rooms. The first—at the top of the stairs—had a camp bed in it and that was all. There wasn't even a sleeping bag on the camp bed, although surely they would be collecting some bedding from the *Cormorant*. The next room was stark empty, opening off from the first, and she stood in the doorway between, biting her lip, thoughtful.

Maybe she had been a shade over-impulsive. It had seemed simple enough. All she had wanted to do was work her passage on the boat, and make Max Routlege admit that she was quite a deckhand. But she had expected to sleep in a cabin with a door that locked.

Not that she had anticipated a need for barricades, but this door hardly swung to, let alone locked. Up here they would hear each other breathing. They might as well be in the same room.

She had expected to be sailing round the coastline, in sight of land and other men and women. Not all alone, on a deserted island, in a cottage with warped doors, with the first man—except dear old Ben—who had ever called her Abbie.

She had asked him to call her that. 'Princess' brought back last night's humiliation, and so did 'Abigail'. But Abbie was an intimacy, although Max Routlege didn't realise it. She wasn't sure that she wanted him calling her Abbie.

Of course she wasn't attracted to him, but when he wasn't being insulting he did have an attractive voice. Deep brown. And she had just said, 'Call me Abbie,' her secret name, the key to her secret self. It would be almost like being called 'Dearest'. Unless of course he went on to say, 'Abbie, you stupid woman ...'

She could hear him up on the roof now, hammering away. 'Abbie my girl,' she said to herself, 'get out there and stop worrying about after dark. You'll probably be so exhausted you'll drop in your tracks and sleep like a baby on the front doorstep.'

Outside, one ladder was up against the side of the house and lashed to the guttering. Max was on a roof ladder, with a pile of tiles on a hod. He hung a tile and nailed it and turned to look down at her as she called, 'Can I bring some tiles up to you?'

'Don't drop them,' he warned her. 'There aren't

74

many spares and there's no getting on the phone for more.'

Everything had to come by sea, of course. She handled them carefully, climbing the ladder with one at a time at first, working her way up to three. That was the most she dared risk as she had to hang on to the ladder. 'Do you nail them all?' she asked.

His answer was muffled, he was holding a nail in the corner of his mouth. 'Every fourth row.'

'That should speed things up,' she said.

He took out the nail and tapped it through the tile into one of the thin wooden slats that ran horizontally across the roofing felt. 'What's the hurry?' he said.

If he had wanted this place renovated fast he wouldn't be doing it himself. He had the money to have the old cottage demolished and a Players' Court built if he'd wanted it. But he was enjoying mending the place with his own hands and she could understand the satisfaction it was giving him, and of course there was no hurry. To go at a leisurely pace would be part of the pleasure.

She had sometimes wondered what the cottage was like that her parents swept away to build their magnificent home on its site. She couldn't imagine her father, or his friends, in a cottage. Unless it was one of those fabulous places that got photographed in super homes magazines.

'No hurry,' she said. 'It doesn't look like rain.'

At first Max had watched her with a patronising tolerance, as though she was a child playing a new game, but after a while a partnership of sorts began to develop. She stayed at the top of the ladder, watching the tiles go on, and as he came down, nearing the guttering so that there were only another two more rows to be laid before the gap was closed, she said, 'Please could I put one on?'

'Why not? It's easy enough. Do you want to hammer or hang?'

'Hammer, please,' she said.

'Get down, then.' She went down the ladder and he followed her. Then she climbed up again, leaned over, hung a tile on its slat, and tapped in the nails through the already prepared holes. She got it on fair and square, and felt quite ridiculously pleased.

Builders had been around often enough at Players' Court, but Abbie's role had only been to see they weren't around when her father came home. This was much more rewarding. She smiled down at the lean tanned face that was watching her half smiling, and said, 'Thank you. I just wanted to put on a token tile so I really have a share in it.'

'You look as though you could use a cup of coffee.'

It was drinking water in the kitchen container, and she said eagerly, 'I'd love one, I thought you'd never ask. You carry on tiling.'

She lit the little gas cooker to boil the kettle, and poured the water on the coffee bags in a mug and a thickish glass—fortunately heatproof. There was powdered milk, she put a spoonful in the glass for herself and brought his out black. 'There's only one mug,' she said.

'I wasn't expecting company. We'll collect some later.'

So they were going back to the boat, if only to collect further essentials. But of course they were, and her mind began to run over what she must bring back with her. A change of clothes, obviously, today's were filthy, what with the heat and the dust. Perhaps they could stay the night on the *Cormorant*. They'd work better tomorrow if they slept in comfortable bunks tonight.

She drank her coffee and Max finished the front tiling, and she helped him carry the ladders round to the back, where the whole thing started all over again, although the hole here was smaller and this too was roof-felted and slatted across.

From the top of the ladder here, by clinging on to the ladder sides and craning round, she almost got a bird's eye view of the island. A stream ran not far behind the cottage, coming down from the western peak; then a multi-coloured plain: green grasses, grey and white rocks, terra-cotta bracken. Beyond the plain was the sea, and the cove where the *Cormorant* was anchored, about half a mile away. 'It's a smashing view up here,' she said.

'Glad you're enjoying it.'

'More than I can ever remember enjoying anything,' she said impulsively.

He started to say something in reply, then changed his mind. She was grimy and happy, and her opinion of Max Routlege was changing. She liked what he was doing here, making himself a home with the seals and the birds. It showed a strong man, with an affinity for weaker things, and enough resources within himself to enjoy solitude.

He had been almost unforgivably rude, unreasonably too, even if he did have bad memories about another girl. But now Abbie was recalling other things he had done in his life, he was a man of action as well as an uncannily perceptive writer, and she thought that even her father would have to agree that this man was real.

That was what Leo Lansing had always said he wanted for his daughter, and Abbie laughed softly at herself for remembering that, and Max looked across at her and asked, 'What's the joke?'

That would be telling. 'Us, up here on the roof,' she said.

'That surprises me too.'

'You said I couldn't surprise you.'

'I was wrong.'

All afternoon the air was alive with birds, and on the beach, and the rocks around the beach, the seals played. Around five o'clock she made cream-cracker chutney and cheese sandwiches, and poured the boiling water on tea-bags this time. They ate at the front of the cottage, Max sitting on a flat stone, Abbie flopped full length, ankles crossed, arms beneath her head.

They watched the seals, and he told her this beach was called Seal Sands. The seals weren't nervous, why should they be? No one would hurt them.

She drank some of her tea, looked at the sun gleaming on the smooth black pelts and said, 'You've got some fantastic pets around. I always wanted a pet.'

'What kind of pet?'

'Nothing exotic. A dog, I always wanted a dog, but my father doesn't like animals.'

Max asked, 'Is he nervous of being upstaged?'

There was the old theatrical cliché about never appearing with a dog or a child, but her father didn't like dogs or children, and when she had asked for a pet a long time ago he had refused flatly. No dogs, no cats. As a child she had pretended she had a large black hound, and stroked a silky head that was only in her imagination.

'So the lady doesn't always get what the lady wants?' said Max, stretching a hand for another biscuit sandwich, and Abbie heard herself saying,

'I don't recollect anyone ever asking what the lady wanted.'

It was a wonderful thing to have a genius for a father. Everything took second place to genius, of course, but no one had ever asked what were her needs or desires.

She was shocked at herself. She was being ungrateful and disloyal, and she closed her eyes and said, 'If I sleep wake me.' She didn't want to go any further with that conversation, but she could feel Max looking at her, and after a while he said,

78

'Why didn't you have freckles before?'

'Because I've been in the sun today without my sun-screen cream on.'

'You should scrap the sun-screen.' A compliment! She sat up and said:

'My goodness, you do improve!'

She was finding it easy to be Abbie, natural and gay. She felt loose-limbed as though even her movements had been constricted before, and the air was reaching her body for the first time.

What Bryan had said yesterday might have been the truth, but today she wasn't a cold fish when the sun was warm enough to bring out a sprinkle of gold freckles on her skin, and she had just got a real compliment out of Max Routlege, and her toes were curling with the satisfaction that gave her.

'So do you,' he said. Improve, he meant. Another compliment, and she laughed.

'I've learned something today, I've hung my first tile, but I don't think this place is going to improve my looks. Look at my hands!'

She held them out for inspection. There were blisters on the palms and the long nails looked incongruous against the short ones that had broken off. 'When I think of the trouble I took,' she said, 'to keep those nails an elegant length, and today I've been snapping them like mad. I should have brought my household gloves along.'

'Household gloves?' he echoed, and she felt it was time he knew a little more about her.

She looped her hands round her ankles, and sat with her chin on her knees, and asked him, 'Who do you think cleans our house?'

He hadn't thought, why should he, it wasn't his establishment. But he had certainly never envisaged Abigail Lansing down on her knees scrubbing any floor. 'Don't you have a treasure of a housekeeper?' he said.

'Maudie's got arthritis,' she told him. 'Sometimes she's crippled with it, and the helps come and go. I do it. Me.' It was a ridiculous thing to keep a secret for years, and now it seemed important that Max should hear it. 'In gloves,' she said. 'By dead of night.'

'*What?*'

She laughed. 'Just like a life of crime, I operate well behind the scenes.' Her eyes were dancing. She was enjoying telling him how far off the mark he had been with her. 'I prepared most of that dinner you ate the other night. I'm a very good cook. Better than Maudie, and she taught me and she says I am.'

'Why didn't you say you'd cooked it?'

The food had been praised. It often was, but Abbie had never laid claim to a dish. 'Well,' she smiled and shrugged, 'it's supposed to be Maudie who does it all.'

'Why?'

She stopped smiling, inspected her jagged nails again and frowned at them this time. 'Because things have to run smoothly for my father. He's a marvellous man. There's no one like him. There isn't, is there?'

'He's a great actor,' said Max. He was frowning a little too. His face was streaked with dust, emphasising the lines that ran from nose to mouth and around the eyes, making him look older and grim.

She had expected his praise of her father, there was no one who didn't agree that Leo Lansing was king, so he would understand why Players' Court had to run without a hitch.

'If my father realised that Maudie can't cope like she used to he'd get in another housekeeper, and goodness knows who we'd get. They don't grow on trees these days—who wants to be somebody else's housekeeper? He'd hate the disruption, and Maudie would hate to have somebody else in charge.' She was sounding as though she was pleading a case, because Max's expression was still rather grim, as though he didn't understand, or didn't approve. 'Why not?' she demanded.

'No reason why not, but why the secrecy? Why shouldn't you cook the dinner?'

'Because my father likes to think I have nothing to do but enjoy myself.'

In future things would be different. She would go on running the house, preparing the meals, coping with the guests, but openly, so that no one could say again that she never did a hand's turn. When she told her father what she had overheard at the party he would agree that she had to change her image a little. It had been horribly humiliating, learning what people said about her behind her back.

Even the writing she did, the pieces for the *Penrann Telegraph*, why shouldn't they be less superficial? Starting with Max, perhaps. Helping Max get this house together would be a livelier celebrity spot than she had ever submitted before.

She would enjoy writing an account of her stay on the island. She was going to enjoy her stay, and she began to ask, 'Would you mind if I wrote about this place?' when she realised he was still frowning. 'What's the matter?' she asked him instead.

'I don't get it,' said Max. 'Doesn't your father know that Maudie's got arthritis?'

'No. He—hates ill-health.' She turned away from his scrutiny and watched the seals again. 'My mother died when she was very young, in an accident, but that might have something to do with it. He can't stand people even feeling off colour around him. I remember once, when I was a child——'

The memories unravelled in her mind. The day when the excitement of his homecoming had brought on a bilious attack in a six-year-old girl. She had lain in bed all day, under Maudie's ministrations, waiting for her father. He had looked in on her quite late, with a few words and an expression of impatience he hadn't bothered to hide. She had been very young, but she had decided then that there must be something unlovable in being ill. She must hide when she was ill or her father wouldn't love her.

She didn't tell Max what she remembered. Her voice trailed away, and she said, 'He's in a very exacting profession. There's a lot of stress in it and he mustn't be worried. Maudie wouldn't have him worried about her for the world. She'd never tell him she isn't young any more, and she wouldn't let me either.'

'It seems a thing he might have noticed,' said Max dryly, and she suspected sarcasm and rushed to her father's defence.

'He's always got so much on his mind. There's always the next part to be lived, because he does live all his roles.'

'To the hilt,' said Max. That didn't sound like unqualified admiration, and suddenly she didn't want to discuss her father with him any more. She got up, asking,

'Are we finishing this roof?' and began to walk round towards the back of the cottage.

They went back to the tiling. She hoped she wouldn't regret having told Max so much, and she made sure he asked no more questions by questioning him about his work. She hadn't read his books, but she had seen television plays, of course, and they talked about them.

'Is this an interview?' he said at last, and she smiled.

'I would like to interview you. The little pieces I've written in my celebrity spot so far have been very milk-and-water. I've always been scared of offending people because they were always our guests.'

'And suddenly you're not? Or do you think I'm too thick-skinned to notice?' He was at the top of the ladder, she at the bottom, and she laughed up at him.

'Hardly, but when I took my little piece into the

office on Friday the editor did say he'd hoped for something a bit livelier about you.'

'How lively?'

She went up with a tile and he reached down for it. 'If I'd been a real journalist,' she said, 'writing a real personality column I'd have asked you about Lady Anne.'

'Of course you would.' He turned away to fix the tile, and she went down the ladder again.

'Are you going to get married?' she asked, surprised at herself, but that was an obvious question for a reporter to ask.

'No.'

'Why not?'

'Perhaps I'm not a marrying man.'

'But she is very much a marrying lady.'

'So the statistics seem to prove. Are you getting married this time?'

'What?' This time? What did he mean by 'this time'?

'Are you marrying Gibson?'

Oh, *Bryan*? 'This time' had sounded as though it was happening now, but Bryan was a long time ago. 'No,' she said.

'Why not?'

She had her foot on the bottom rung of the ladder, and her pale pink toenails gleamed through the dust. 'Do we get some hot washing water tonight?' she asked. 'When we go back to the *Cormorant* wouldn't it be more sensible to sleep there? Even though the roof's fixed this place isn't really habitable yet, is it?'

'You've got a point. Why aren't you marrying your latest?'

He wasn't looking at her, that was something. She could have said, 'I'm not a marrying lady,' which seemed to be true. But she found herself saying, 'I don't want to marry Bryan. I don't love him. I liked him, though, until last night when I heard him telling somebody that I was a frigid fish but it couldn't hurt to be seen around with King Leo's daughter.'

Max was hammering and went on hammering for several seconds. Then he asked, 'Is that why you're running?'

She shrugged, which was no answer because he had his back to her. 'I'm not running,' she said, 'I'm marooned, I'm not going anywhere.' She heard her own laughter, and realised that it hadn't hurt too much, repeating what Bryan had said. She said, 'We went to this party, and he asked me to dress up, put on some of the famous jewels. I was a knockout—well, my pearls were. Bryan was proud of me.'

Max looked down at her and grinned. 'Bryan should see you now,' he said.

'Shouldn't he just?'

'A lot of people should see you now.'

'A lot of people wouldn't recognise me.' Maybe not even Maudie. Her father would think she had gone crazy. He wanted her to be beautiful. He would *not* approve, but Max did. Max laughed and said:

'We could both do with a clean-up, but I think you look fine.'

'So do you.' They were laughing, fooling, and she was free as a bird, and she almost believed she could fly.

They finished the roof in the early evening and while Max stacked the ladders and put away the tools Abbie walked round the cottage. 'That's a handsome roof you've got there,' she said.

'Glad you like it,' he said.

'Do you know how much builders charge? The builders are in at Players' Court.' Why didn't she say 'at home'? Players' Court was her home, so why was she referring to it as though it was just a building somewhere? 'They're costing a fortune,' she went on.

84

'You could earn a good living as a builder. Have you ever thought of that?'

'It's a thought.' It was a load of nonsense, who would ever have imagined that she could be talking such nonsense with Max Routlege? 'Have you ever thought of turning builder's mate?'

'Is this an offer?'

'We're a good team.'

'The best. I'll consider it, very seriously.' Laughter had a lovely sound, mingling with the sound of the sea and the sound of the birds. She thought—if I could write music I'd catch this moment. 'Back to comparative luxury now, then?' she said.

'That's it.'

Rowing round the peak to the cove on the other side of the island where the *Cormorant* was anchored, 'It's a straight walk across, isn't it?' she asked. 'Not much of a walk?'

'About half a mile.'

'I think I'd like to walk. Could you pick me up in the cove? Could I get down?'

'It's easier to get down there than it is in Players' Court bay. I'll come across when I see you. I'll start a meal going.' He grinned. 'Are you sure you can cook and you're not dodging galley duty?'

'You'll have to take my word for it until tomorrow.' She nodded mischievously, 'That's it, you cook the first meal and then I'll see what your standards are.'

'Rough and ready.'

'And that's only the cooking?' she teased.

She watched the dinghy until it was out of sight. When it vanished behind the peak she was alone. There was no one else on the island, nor on the sea within her line of vision.

She had never been physically alone before. Even when her father was away from Players' Court and there was no stream of guests she had always been in contact with crowds, through the mail that came for her father, and in the eyes that followed her wherever she went because she was Leo Lansing's daughter.

You don't care about that, do you? she thought, looking at the birds and the seals. You've never heard of King Leo. King Leo would not approve of his princess as a builder's mate, but it was a handsome roof.

Max was a handsome man. She had seen some famous torsos in her time, stripped off round their swimming pool, but she had never spent so long looking at any one man as she had done today, perched on top of a ladder, watching him mend a roof.

He was copper-brown. So were lots of famous torsos, but she had watched his muscles ripple as he hammered or reached. Broad shoulders and narrow waist, flat stomach, and a hard and handsome face. If she had been able to draw she could have sketched him very well from memory.

Many of the men she met were handsome, looks didn't count for much. The exciting thing about Max was that his character should reveal such unexpected facets. This morning she had disliked him. This evening she liked him immensely. One surprising day had done that, and it had been just as surprising for Max, which doubled the pleasure.

Only last night she had been choosing her dress to go to the party with Bryan. Abigail Lansing, wearing her pearls, was the girl Bryan wanted to take to the party.

He wouldn't care for Abbie. She didn't know who would, except Maudie and Ben. And Max. Max did, and he was preparing a meal which they would eat at the teak table in the *Cormorant*'s little saloon tonight.

This was the best day I have ever known, she thought. I'm having more fun than I can ever remember having. It was as though all the bubbling youth and vitality that had been held in check, so that no one could say

Leo Lansing's daughter was less than a credit to him, was fizzing in her veins.

She felt wonderful. She looked at the cottage again. It was going to make a good home, secure against winter storms, cool in the summer's heat. The island was a bird sanctuary, a seal sanctuary. A sanctuary was a place where nothing could hurt you. No one hurt the seals here, Max had said, and that was what a home should be.

She turned to head for the stream, to cross the island to the cove. It was not her home. Her home was her fathers' house, but she believed at that moment that it was. As though she had a claim to it as natural as breathing, as loving, as though she had come here to claim what was hers.

CHAPTER FIVE

ABBIE reached the stream, that came cascading down from the heights, beneath which the birds nested, to cross the plain and reach the sea. The water was shallow and diamond-clear, so that the pebbles on the bed of the stream were in jewelled colours: coral pink and agate, jet and tiger's eye and amethyst. They were only pebbles, but they were as bright as any of her jewels.

The sun had gone down behind the western peak, where the sky was burning red and high jagged rocks stood stark and dark on the skyline.

She cupped her hands and drank from the stream, splashing the sparkling water over her face. Then she sat there for a little while, looking at the sunset. She could have stayed happily for hours. It was so peaceful, so beautiful. But Max would be wondering what had happened to her, and she was ravenously hungry, and she had plenty of days to watch sunsets, and explore the island.

She would climb the peaks, going quietly so that the birds were not disturbed, seeing how many types of birds she recognised. She would ask Max if he knew what birds lived here. She would ask him to come with her.

That would be best, to ask Max to come too. She would like to share this solitude with him. They had talked today and the talking had been so easy that she thought that silence might be easy too. That they could have sat here together, watching the sunset, and said nothing and been at peace.

She smiled wryly at herself. I miss him, she thought. The man I disliked yesterday, and feared a little this morning—when I knew I was going to be here alone with him—now I miss him.

She got up, brushing grass from her jeans. If she missed him she had better get along to him. And she had better watch what she was about. She had felt abandoned by Bryan, left vulnerable, and Max Routlege's approval was a fine ego-booster. His more-than-approval would show them all, herself included, that she was desirable as a woman to one of the most eligible men in the country. To a man with a name as well known as her father's.

But as she had no experience in this game, and as she might find it wasn't a game but something as real as life and death, she had better watch her step. She must get back to the *Cormorant* now, walking briskly but calmly, and ignoring the fact that her heart was racing as though there was a lover waiting for her, over there in the bay.

All the same she spotted the *Cormorant* with a smug little smile, and told herself it was such a nice-looking boat that the sight of it gave her pleasure, that was why she was smiling like a Cheshire cat.

The dinghy was alongside, so Max was aboard, and as there was no sign of him he must be below deck. He'd said he'd get a meal on, and he'd said she could get down into the cove.

The cliffs shelved, steep but not sheer, and she clambered down towards the water level, finding a crag of rock jutting into a natural jetty where she could sit and wait to be seen.

Here I am, she thought, sitting on a rock again, waiting for a lift to the *Cormorant*. Except that this was not at all like the last time. Last time there was storm in every way, and now she was warm, relaxed and happy. But sticky and dirty too, and *why* was she sitting here?

It would only take a few minutes to swim across, and

a swim would be the next best thing to a bath. She was out of her shirt, jeans and sandals, in seconds. She slipped her watch into her jeans pocket and slid into the water.

The water was deep and green and flecked with fire from the sunset. The bay was ringed with the sharp-pointed rocks, you'd have to know your course through them to bring a boat into here. They looked like teeth, like a set of monolithic jaws.

'Snap!' she carolled idiotically, and waved as Max appeared at the rail. 'Dinner ready?' she called.

'Watch out, there are rocks!' he shouted back, and as he spoke she felt a cold searing pain against her kicking leg.

She went on swimming. The ache was dull, she wouldn't really feel it until she got out of the water. Maybe it wasn't much, but she daren't look. It was bad enough to see the sunset on the water, without checking if she was leaving a scarlet trail behind her.

Max was coming down into the dinghy, but she reached it almost before he did, and clung to the ladder. 'I swam across a rock,' she gasped. He came over the side to help her, lifting her into the dinghy. 'I don't know what I've done.' She looked round at the swathe of graze on her leg, that dabbled with blood as she watched it. 'Ouch!' she said.

It could have been worse, a deeper gash that would have needed stitches, but this was smarting enough to bring tears to her eyes when she blinked the sea-water from her lashes.

She climbed the ladder, and winced as she went over on to the deck. Max had followed close behind. His hands were on her arms again, but this time in support as he asked her, 'Sure you're all right?'

'I'm not going to faint, if that's what you mean.'

'Yes, I suppose it was what I meant. But of course

you're not going to faint. Let's get you below. Hang on.'

She could probably have hopped, but he picked her up and she clung to him awkwardly, avoiding contact for her graze, which was bleeding profusely now and hurting like crazy. It wasn't simple for him, negotiating the hatchway and the passageway and the narrow steps with a girl who had one stiff leg stuck out as though it was made of wood.

But they got down into the saloon, and she sat on one of the settees, and Max put a big square biscuit tin under her foot. 'All right?' he said again.

'Mmm. It needs bathing, I suppose.'

He brought a first aid kit from one of the fore-cabins, and a bowl of water from the sink, and asked her, 'Can you manage?'

Her head was a little muzzy and she wished she could lean back and close her eyes and say, 'You do it, I don't want to look.' But it was only a graze, although a deep one.

'Yes,' she said.

She swabbed it with a cotton wool swab, and grimaced as the antiseptic stung. 'You wouldn't have a bullet I could bite on, would you?'

'I'll get you a drink,' he said.

'Please, I don't like rum. I know you gave it me last time and it warmed me up very nicely, but I do hate the stuff.'

'Why didn't you say?' He was pouring something else, and she laughed a little jerkily.

'I was scared of you, I suppose. You're fairly terrifying when you're being insulting.'

'Sorry about that.' He brought her brandy and said, 'Whether you like this or not, get it down, there's a good girl.'

Abbie gulped a little, and he took the cotton wool swab from her and knelt beside her. 'It's a nasty graze,'

91

he said. 'But it's clean enough. We'll put something on it and you can rest it up tonight. See how you feel in the morning about seeing a doctor.'

Her heart sank oddly. He was offering to take her back and she didn't want to go, certainly not for a stupid little thing like this. She said, 'I'll be fine in the morning. I heal very quickly.'

He grinned up at her. 'Is that the brandy talking?'

'Not yet.' His wet hair was thick, brown and sun-streaked, and she would have liked to run her fingers through it.

He dabbed on something cooling and soothing, covered the graze with lint and bandage. He was deft and careful, and she felt that if something much worse than this happened to her Max could have put it right. Her voice wobbled a little. 'I can see I did right, signing on as your crew.'

'Why did you?' He put the biscuit tin back under her foot. 'Why this boat for a change of scene?'

'It wasn't the boat, it was you.' She sipped some more brandy. 'No one ever told me to my face before that I was useless, although that was the general opinion. I felt if I could get you to change your mind—it would —well, give me a bit of self-respect.' She went on with brittle gaiety, 'You said I was nothing, but you'll have to take that back, because nothing can't bleed.'

'I take it back.' She finished her brandy, but the glow she felt was from his admission. He took the empty glass from her and said, 'Emphatically you are some-thing.'

'You too.' She was so sharply aware of him that it was almost a relief when he turned away and went out of the saloon. Although he returned almost immediately, carrying a large bath towel, telling her,

'Get your wet things off and wrap this round you.' Then he went again, and Abbie got out of her sea-soaked bra and pants and huddled into the soft white folds. Her leg hurt, but not too much, and this was like being tucked up beneath blankets in bed.

She could smell food, curry—she hoped Max wasn't one of those who thinks a good curry should skin the roof of your mouth, because she was hungry. And drowsy, from the brandy and the day's work and the excitement of everything. She snuggled into the corner of the settee, her feet on the biscuit tin, and floated into sleep.

When she woke she thought for a moment it was morning because daylight still streamed through the portholes, and she was refreshed as though she had had hours of rest. Her surroundings didn't surprise her. She didn't have even a second's uncertainty, no looking around and wondering where on earth she was. She opened her eyes and saw Max in the galley, and sniffed to see if the smell was breakfast, but it was still curry.

He was cleaned up, wearing a red and white check shirt now and quite well pressed pants, although he was still barefoot, and Abbie glanced down hastily at herself, thankful to find she hadn't tossed off her coverings in her sleep but was still cocooned in towelling.

'Is it morning?' she asked.

'Not by a long way.' He turned and smiled at her.

'How long have I been asleep?'

'All of thirty minutes.'

She was surprised but pleased, it meant she hadn't missed the evening. She said cheerfully, 'If you ply young ladies with strong drink you must expect them to flake out on you.'

'Or dive overboard?' he grinned. 'And I resent the suggestion that I make a habit of plying young ladies with anything. In your case this seems to be turning into a hospital ship. You should be grateful I offer you my good liquor instead of making cracks about it.'

'I'm grateful,' she said. 'Honestly, I'm grateful. Are you going to feed the patient?'

'Coming right up.'

She sat up and had second thoughts. 'Would it wait a few more minutes?'

'Why?'

'I don't feel dressed for dinner.'

He laughed and offered, 'I'll get you some safety pins.'

'I need a wash.'

'I'll get you a bowl of water.'

'And I need the loo.'

'Just through there.' He pointed to the door to the fore cabins and she shook her head.

'I do want to go to my own cabin. I want to get dressed. I know I'm decent enough in this, but I feel like a bale of cotton.'

'All right. But don't put your weight on your leg.' She put a hand on his shoulder, and clutched her trailing towel around her with the other, and shuffled up the steps and along the companionway between the saloon and her cabin. She said,

'You've had something to eat, haven't you? I mean, you're not waiting for your dinner?'

'I'm going back now to finish off half a pound of cold sausages,' he said.

Once inside the cabin Abbie dropped the towel and hopped to a bunk. She wasn't going to spend the evening looking a wreck. She was going to make herself as presentable as possible in the clothes she had brought.

If anyone had told her this morning, when she was packing, that she would regret not including a pretty dress she would have said they were crazy. But she did regret it, and now she had to work out how to make herself look fetching in strictly practical gear.

She washed, in the little toilet cubicle, undoing her hair from the bedraggled ribbon that had fastened it back and washing her hair too. The water was cold, but at least it swilled away the salt and dust, and she towelled it briskly and hoped it would dry in a natural wave. She had a natural wave, but her hair had always been professionally washed and styled, smoothed and pampered.

She made up, with lipstick and eye-shadow. Habit had made her bring along her make-up, although she hadn't expected to be peering so anxiously into the mirror as she applied it.

Not too bad, she thought. I don't look beautiful, and I don't look expensive, but I do look healthy.

She had pink cheeks where the sun had caught her cheekbones, and freckles, and her eyes were very bright. There was a sparkle about her that was new and transforming.

She put on a white cheesecloth blouse, a blue denim skirt, and a pair of rubber-soled shoes she had selected for deck wear. Then she filed down all her fingernails to a uniform length and went back to the saloon, using handrails and edging along the wall. Because her leg wasn't feeling too bad at all and she was anxious to give it every consideration.

The table between the settees was laid for two. Max was reading a book, and he stood up as she opened the door. Something melted in her because he came and helped her to her seat. She had had surface courtesies all her life, but this was different. No one had carried her before, when she was hurt, as he had carried her.

Unless she counted Ben, when she fell from a tree as a child and Ben had carried her in to Maudie and her governess.

She had been bruised, they had made a fuss of her, but when her father heard that night he had said, 'What's the child doing climbing trees? I don't want her growing into a hoyden.' She hadn't known what a hoyden was, but he hadn't asked if she had been hurt and she had climbed no more trees.

'Curry,' said Max. 'If you don't like it there's a good

selection of tins, and the cold sausages and cheese.'

'I like it,' she said.

He put a plate of rice, topped with a curry and a pink sprinkle of paprika, in front of her, and she dug in with a fork, relieved to find it didn't scald her tongue. It was very palatable and she made small complimentary sounds, 'Mmm, *yes.*' She scooped some chutney from a jar beside her plate, and asked, 'How do you make it?'

'This time it was onions, a tin of condensed chicken soup, some yoghurt and a large tin of shrimps. Not forgetting the curry powder.'

'Well, tonight's version is a winner.' She ate on, nodding approval.

'For that,' he said, 'you shall have a glass of wine and I'll overlook what you said about me plying my victims with alcohol.'

He poured two glasses from the bottle on the table, and Abbie backed in mock apprehension. 'I didn't say they were victims. Now you've got me worried.'

'You're something of a worry yourself.' He looked at her, over his glass. 'Why couldn't you wait until I came up on deck? Why did you have to start swimming for it?'

'It wasn't far,' she explained, 'and the water looked lovely.'

'I suppose I should have warned you that swimming's out just there. It's all right the other side, off the sands.' He grinned ruefully. 'I can tell you I sweated when I saw you!'

'Sorry,' she said meekly. 'I won't do it again.'

Max started on his own plate of curry, telling her, 'After I'd left you I began to wonder if I should have let you walk across the island on your own.'

'You don't have tigers, do you?' She was elated by his concern, it warmed her. He chuckled.

'There was nothing about tigers in the sales contract,

96

but there are a few natural hazards. You have to watch your step.' Odd he should say that, that was what she had been thinking as she walked across the island, but not the way he meant it. 'Watch out for chimneys,' he said.

She knew about them. They were funnels in the rock, sometimes covered over by bracken or fern or gorse. If you stepped on them down you went, maybe all the way to the outlet over the sea. Sometimes the wind got in them and made a weird howling. Sometimes high tides entered the lower end with a roar, sending spray all the way up, to burst spectacularly on higher ground. 'I'll watch out for chimneys,' she said. 'The stream was beautiful.'

'There are two of them, one from each peak.'

'With coloured pebbles on the bed.' She had a bright idea. 'I'll collect some pebbles while I'm here and have them polished for a bracelet when I——' She hesitated. 'When I get home' didn't sound right. 'When I go away from here,' she said, and Max asked,

'What do you want with polished pebbles, the collection of stones you've got?'

So that she could touch each pebble and remember exactly where she found it. It would be better than photographs because the pictures would be in her mind. She had no fear that time might dim them. 'Why not?' she said. 'My jewellery is a liability, although it's insured. I'd like a bracelet of pebbles.'

'It's a modest ambition.'

'I could start a collection of pebbles, and shells.' She was making rapid inroads in her curry, and she took a few sips of wine before she told him, 'I've never collected anything before.'

'Harking back to your jewellery,' said Max, 'what's that if it isn't a collection?'

'I didn't collect that. My father chose it. I never really wanted it.'

She spoke without thought, immediately regretting it, so that she said emphatically, 'My father is very generous, I've got some very beautiful things.'

'They get a lot of press coverage,' said Max.

'Anything to do with my father usually does.' Her hair was drying soft and floppy, she pushed it back and smiled. 'But he gets on all right with most reporters.'

'He knows the value of publicity,' said Max.

'Well, he's a public figure and the public want to know about him.'

'That's right.'

She always talked about her father, it was what most people wanted to hear, and although she was making a stand for a personal identity now she still adored him with unquestioning starry-eyed devotion.

So she talked about Leo and Max listened, and read between the lines because that was the kind of mind he had. Attuned to the unobvious. That was why his writing cut deep. If he hadn't been a writer he would have made an implacably aggressive prosecuting attorney.

At last Abbie began to laugh at herself. 'Listen to me! I got so mad because they said I was only King Leo's daughter, but I still know I've got the most fantastic father in the world.'

'You do, don't you?' said Max quietly, and still smiling she asked,

'What are your parents like?'

'Dead. A long time ago.'

'Oh, I'm sorry. Do you remember them?'

'No.'

'Who looked after you?' He was a man so capable of looking after himself that it seemed a silly question, but a long time ago he had been a child.

'The local authority.'

She said again, 'I'm sorry' and he grinned.

'Any sympathy should go to them. I was a natural street fighter.'

He was a success now. Almost as famous as her father, probably richer. 'How did you start?' she asked, and she would have listened happily to a detailed account of his struggle for fame, but he said,

'I'll lend you the book.'

Abbie had read newspaper stories about him, but she hadn't read his books and she said, 'When I get back I'll read them all.'

He laughed. 'I wouldn't wish that on you.'

'What are you writing now?'

'I'm not,' he said. 'The idea's still in my head. I'm giving myself another couple of weeks' break, then getting down to the serious work.'

'Where?'

'I don't know.'

She thought it more likely that he wasn't telling her. Any more than he was prepared to confide the theme of his next book or play, and she was anxious not to intrude. Theirs was a very new relationship, privacy must be respected.

Time passed quickly. They sat with fruit for dessert, and a large pot of coffee on the table, talking until Max got up and lit the lamp, and afterwards until he said, 'We should be turning in.'

Tomorrow he was repairing floorboards in the bedrooms. He'd told her she would be taking it easy, but she'd decide about that when morning came. 'Who washes up?' she asked.

There wasn't much. 'I do,' he said.

She smiled a wide and happy smile. 'Well, I did the clearing up after the dinner I cooked for you at Players' Court.'

'Did you? That night?'

'Yes, after they'd all gone to bed. My father told me to run along and get my beauty sleep, and I covered

99

that smashing dress with the housecoat I keep for covering smashing dresses, and did the washing up and tidied the dining and drawing rooms.'

'So that everyone believed old Maudie had done it?'

'Yes.'

He leaned back, his voice terse instead of amused as she had expected him to be. 'What a bloody silly pantomime,' he said.

After a moment she said, 'I suppose it was.'

Of course it was. All that planning and scheming to put on a front of being one of the beautiful, useless people, and perhaps Max was annoyed that he had made an error of judgment in her case, and disliked her harping on it.

She stood up, putting most of the weight on her good leg. 'Goodnight,' she said, 'and I enjoyed the curry.'

His grin made up for that flash of irritation, making her smile too. 'I'll try to remember the recipe.' He got up and came round to her. 'Now, are you fit to walk?'

'Fit to dance,' she said lightly. The leg had stopped aching some time ago. She wasn't sure when, but she had almost forgotten her injury.

'No dancing tonight,' said Max. 'I'll see you to your cabin.'

She had got here from her cabin, she could have got herself back, but it was nicer to be helped, and he picked up a torch and they joked again about her treating the *Cormorant* as a hospital ship.

Her door was open when they reached it. Max gave her the torch, and she leaned against the door jamb as he took his arm from around her waist. She had a hand on his shoulder. She could manage now, he was going now, but she loosed him slowly. Her fingers felt as though they were slipping from a rock and closing on empty air.

Suddenly he took her hand and held it, palm to palm, and she clutched at him convulsively while his grip tightened. In the light of the torch she looked at their entwined hands, the gleaming whiteness of her knuckles, the darkness of his skin against hers.

'Goodnight,' he said at last, and retraced his steps down the little corridor.

'Sleep well,' she called after him.

Inside the cabin she pressed the back of her hand to her lips, and she was trembling. What was that? A handshake or a kiss? Something of both, an offering and taking. She had never before held a man's hand and felt the earth shake.

This was a boat and the sturdy fibreglass hull wasn't shaking, it was rocking very gently, but the shaking was inside her. And when Max said goodnight his voice was strained as though he found it no easier to break the clasp of their fingers than she had.

Abbie sat down heavily on her bunk, took off her shoes, then her blouse, fumbling with the buttons and the zip of her skirt. It was hot as a tropical night in here. She wouldn't bother to light the little gas lamp. She could see enough by the torch to get undressed, sponge hands and face, and find her nightdress in the top of the locker between the bunks.

After she turned off the torch it took only a few minutes before her eyes accustomed themselves to the darkness, and the starlight and moonlight that came through the porthole seemed brighter than the torch had been.

She lay a little awkwardly because of her leg. On her side, her head on one arm, the other arm flung across her. It was a comfortable bunk, but she couldn't rest. The sound of the sea should have lulled her, it did at Players' Court, and here it was rocking her as well as singing to her, but sleep wouldn't come.

Max should be asleep by now. She wondered what his cabin was like, how he looked when he slept. She remembered an article she had read somewhere that claimed you could tell people's character by their sleeping posture. If you slept on your back you were confident, successful, sure of your place in the sun. That had to be Max.

If you curled up awkwardly, as she was doing, it meant you were a timid soul, depressed about almost everything. Although it could also mean that you had swum over a rock recently, and had a large pad of lint attached to you by several feet of neatly applied bandage.

And as the experts also claimed that everyone changed positions dozens of times during a good night's sleep it must also mean that you could start off confident and successful, and finish a curled-up, browned-off mouse.

In the morning she would tell Max what she had been lying here thinking about. It should make him smile. But then she thought again, because inquiring about a man's sleeping habits might be misunderstood when there were only the two of you on this little boat, on this little island.

She laughed softly to herself. What would people think about this? They'd never believe it of Abigail Lansing. Other girls went out and found their own adventures, but Abigail's had always been handed to her, like her jewels, by her father.

What would Bryan think when he heard? She was harbouring no resentment against Bryan. There was no bitterness left. Nor for the other men who had tired of her and gone away. No hurt even, now, from Stephen.

If she had really cared about Stephen she wouldn't have let him go like that. He had been quiet that evening, he had had something on his mind, and Abbie had recognised the signs with a sinking feeling of helplessness.

He was tiring of her already. As soon as this he had realised that he didn't want to get deeper involved with her, and she had retreated behind her façade of cool elegance, playing the hostess as she always did, to the glittering crowd of her father's guests.

When Stephen said goodnight he told her he'd been offered a lift to London where there were some friends he should contact, some business to see to. Abbie had listened to his embarrassed explanations, keeping her eyes from the girl who hovered, and with whom Stephen had spent a good part of the evening. She had said, of course, and he must keep in touch, and she would be away herself next week. Her father was taking her to Paris.

That morning her father had asked her if she would like a few days in Paris, so there it was, a readymade comeback.

She had heard no more of Stephen. She had returned from Paris with some beautiful clothes, and she had had a lovely holiday. Her father wouldn't let her mope. 'If he went off with Ginny Williams,' her father said, 'that's the last anybody will hear of him. She'll eat the poor fellow alive. You didn't want him, princess. One of these days we'll find you a real man.'

But if she had cared enough about Stephen she wouldn't have gone to Paris, and she would have moved in when Ginny Williams was talking so confidentially to him in corners.

I never cared for any of them, she realised. I never wanted them enough. Like her father said, they weren't real.

Nothing had ever been like this time. Max had asked her, 'Are you getting married this time?' and the question had confused her because 'this time' was no longer Bryan. It was Max, and for the first time she would fight to have and to hold ...

Although the porthole was fully open the air in the little cabin was oppressively hot when she fell asleep, and when she woke. She was lying on top of the bedding, but she still felt half suffocated, and she sat up, pushing her fingers into her hair and holding it off her face.

Her porthole faced the open sea, with a glimpse of encircling cliffs either side and a sky full of stars, and she went across to the other bunk under the porthole to breathe the fresher air. Now she was fully awake she could lie gasping down here for hours before she fell asleep again. Up on deck it would be cooler, and she could see the island by night, while the birds and the seals slept.

The thought was irresistible. Abbie slipped on a light kimono, and she was at the door of her cabin before a twinge of pain reminded her of her swimming mishap. When it did she was pleased, it meant she was far from being incapacitated, she was moving around quite comfortably. Tomorrow—today, she had no idea what the time was—she should be able to help in the cottage. She might clean down the inside walls in preparation for some of that paint that was being stored in the kitchen.

Max's cabin was below the foredeck, with a skylight. The skylight was opaque, but he would surely have it open tonight, so she would stay well away from it and make no noise. She crept softly, her bare feet almost soundless, and stood by the rail astern, looking at the dark irregular shape of the island.

It was ghostly under the moon, and there was a little breeze up here that lifted her hair and touched her face like light cool fingers. She sat on the deck, her knees hunched, resting her chin on the lower rail, feeling wonderfully soothed and tranquil.

She must have been there about five minutes when she realised she wasn't alone on deck, and she raised her head as Max came towards her.

'It's cooler here,' she said.

'You're all right?'

'Oh yes, the leg doesn't hurt at all. What are you doing here?'

'I often sleep on deck.'

So he had been up here all the time. She almost said, 'I hope I didn't disturb you,' but somehow she felt that she hadn't, any more than he spoiled the serenity for her. She was glad he was here. She said, 'It's magical by moonlight, your island. Like the island in Shakespeare's *Tempest*.' As he smiled she looked at him through her soft loose hair, suggesting gaily, 'Perhaps we're Prospero and Miranda?'

'As one Miranda was a princess and another a mermaid you could well be a Miranda,' he said.

'And as you have a magic island you should be Prospero.' Tall and strong and powerful, but old, so that wasn't Max. He laughed and asked,

'How many fathers do you want?'

The last thing she wanted was to be a daughter to Max, so she laughed too, hugging her knees.

'I think I've got the wrong cast list.'

'I could always be Caliban.'

'The monster?' She acted shocked surprise. 'The demi-devil?'

'I've always felt that Caliban had a bad deal. Turned into a one-man chain-gang for making a pass at Miranda.' He stood with his back to the rail. Behind him, in the dark waters of the cove, the sharp pointed rocks glittered. 'Strictly speaking the island was Caliban's,' said Max. 'He should have been nobody's slave.'

'So it was,' she gurgled. 'Caliban was there first, wasn't he?' Then the raillery left her and she sighed at the wonder around them. 'It's a beautiful night,' she said.

'Yes.' Max sounded suddenly brisk. 'If you're staying up here I'll get you something more comfortable than the deck.'

He brought a canvas recliner chair from below, and

as Abbie sat down she asked, 'Are you staying on deck?'

'Yes. Back to my air mattress yonder. It's late and breakfast's early. Goodnight again.'

She leaned her head on the padded headrest and listened to his footsteps going towards the other end of the boat. If he had brought another chair for himself they could have talked a little longer, then slept. Not talking, not touching, simply companionably close.

Of course a mattress was more relaxing, and he needed relaxed sleep if he was to spend tomorrow prying up and nailing down floorboards. Abbie skirted the suspicion that he had stayed as long as they were talking lightly, and left when she sighed sentimentally. There had been no tight holding of hands with this goodnight, but Max had brought her a recliner and made her comfortable, and if she raised her voice he would hear what she called.

She wasn't likely to call. What could she call? 'Are you there? Are you asleep? Would you mind if I paddled the dinghy out to collect my clothes and my watch from that jutting-out shelf of rock over there. Dear Caliban, would you mind if I fell in love with you?'

There was nothing that she could call, and she lay listening to the sea, and very soon she fell asleep.

She woke when Max touched her and said, 'It's turning chilly. You'd do better in your bunk.'

Abbie felt the chill in the air as she opened her eyes. There had been a sharp drop in temperature that would have woken her soon. She sat up and shivered. 'Wh—where did the heatwave go?'

'Where heatwaves often go at three in the morning,' said Max. 'You don't do much sleeping out of doors, do you?'

'My first night under the stars,' she said. 'Next time I'll bring a blanket. See you in four hours.'

It was turning into a disturbed night, and when she got into her bunk and snuggled down she fell into her deepest slumber. If Max hadn't rapped on her door at about half past seven she would have slept much longer. As it was she woke woozy. She knew where she was, no question about that, but her eyelids were heavy and she could hardly get out 'All right!' for yawning.

'Tea,' he said. 'Can I bring it in?'

'Please.'

He handed her a mug and asked, 'How's the leg?'

'I don't know. It hasn't woken up yet.'

'Breakfast's ready when you are.'

She'd drink her tea and then she'd be ready. 'Another good day,' said Max.

'I'm sure it will be,' smiled Abbie.

They paddled in to the jetty of rock to collect her clothes—it was her watch she wanted—and then round the peak to Seal Sands and the cottage.

She did what she had planned, started cleaning up the walls, brushing off the loose flakes of white paint. 'Can I light a fire in this fireplace?' she called up to Max. 'I want some hot water to wash down the walls.'

His face appeared between the ceiling beams. 'Better not until I've checked the chimney, and take it easy, will you? I don't know that you should be standing on that leg.'

'It isn't hurting. It was only a scrape.' It was stiff rather than painful today, so long as she remembered not to knock it or stride out, and to sit down carefully.

She heated water on the Calor gas and when she had the living room and the little kitchen ready for their coat of paint tomorrow she went upstairs and sat on the camp bed, and talked to Max. He was making a good job of the bedroom floors.

They were going back to the *Cormorant* again that evening, but today she hoped the cottage would be habitable before their stay was over. It would be fun to light the lamp here at night, to cook and eat a real meal. Max might bring other friends here, but if Abbie was the first woman that should improve her chances of staying the first, the one who mattered most. She hoped with increasing fervour that this partnership would last.

They went down to the sands during the afternoon, sitting still and quiet in the shade of a small cluster of rocks while the seals came closer, lolloping around them.

She picked up a smooth white pebble that should polish like marble. She could have found a more colourful one if she had searched farther, but she wanted pebbles for each day, and she wasn't too mobile today, so this was the first of her collection.

Max laughed at her, but he said, 'I'll have them strung for you, if you still fancy wearing pebbles when you leave here.'

'If you have them made into a bracelet for me,' she said impulsively, 'I'll wear it rather than diamonds.' She flushed when she'd said that and hoped he wouldn't realise how serious she was.

'I never heard tell that pebbles were a girl's best friend,' he said drily. 'And I doubt if your father would approve of you disparaging your diamonds.'

There was often something in his voice when he spoke of her father that she couldn't understand. He admired her father, he had said Leo Lansing was a great actor, and her father respected Max's work. The two most important men in her life must like each other. Anything else was unthinkable, and she wouldn't think about it.

'Diamonds can be a nuisance,' she said, picking up a shell pink stone and wrapping that in the tissue with the stone that was going to look like marble. 'Mine go in and out of the bank vaults like yo-yos. Maudie was getting Ben to take them into Penrann for me yesterday.'

'Who's Ben?' drawled Max.

He was sitting, loose-limbed and relaxed, back against a rock. He wasted no energy, which was probably why he achieved so much. Most of the time even his voice sounded lazy.

'Our gardener,' said Abbie. 'He's been with us as long as I can remember.'

'Another old retainer?'

She smiled. 'Like Maudie? Yes, I suppose so. It sounds very Victorian, doesn't it?'

'Do you work in the garden as well?'

'Sometimes. Ben doesn't need helping like Maudie does. He's very fit.'

'Good for Ben,' said Max. 'Do they know you're with me?'

'I told Maudie I was going down to the harbour to see if you'd take me aboard.' She looked sideways at him, apprehension clenching her stomach muscles. 'I didn't know how long I'd be away then, of course, just a day or two, I thought. Do you mind them knowing I'm with you?'

'Why should I mind? I wondered if you should phone, or send a card. We don't want them worrying if you've sunk without trace.'

'You're nice,' she said, and looked at the strong face and thought—nice as the rocks, as the storm, what a silly word to apply to a man like Max. She laughed at herself and said, 'Well, it's a nice thought.'

'I do have nice thoughts occasionally.' He leered, 'But most of them are the other sort,' and Abbie went into a little gale of giggles.

'Anyhow, how can I send Maudie a postcard?' she said.

'From St Ives. We could go there in the morning.'

'And come back?' she inquired quickly, anxiously.

'We could come right back.'

'I won't say where this island is, I'll just say I'm on the *Cormorant*.' She took a handful of dry soft sand

and let it trickle between her fingers. As it did she said slowly, 'Will Lady Anne mind?'

'No.'

'She won't mind you sailing off, and vanishing for a fortnight with another girl?' When he didn't answer at once she said awkwardly, 'Isn't she—supposed to be——?'

'What?'

'Well, your very good friend. Isn't she?'

'A very good friend,' he said, 'who's still in love with her first husband. She shouldn't have made him divorce her. If she ever gets him back they might even make a go of it.'

That was interesting and welcome news, but she still had to ask, 'Are you in love with her?'

'No.' He didn't sound as though he ever had been. He sounded amused.

'Because I wouldn't like to cause any trouble.'

'Abbie——' Max said abruptly.

'Yes?' She felt a nerve flutter in the base of her throat. He looked so stern that she was frightened. His eyes held hers for a moment, hard and probing, then he said,

'Forget it. It doesn't matter.' He began to talk about their trip to the mainland in the morning, where they could have lunch in St Ives, and she nodded, listening, although all she wanted to do was say,

'Tell me what you were thinking just now. Tell me what's going to go wrong.'

CHAPTER SIX

ABBIE got dinner on the *Cormorant* that night. It was homely enough—cottage pie with a tin of mince, a can of tomatoes, dried onions and instant mashed potatoes. But she mashed the potato with butter and cheese, and sprinkled the top with Parmesan and dabbed it with butter, and it came out of the oven after forty minutes looking and smelling appetising.

Afterwards Abbie said, 'If I wasn't here, what would you be doing now?'

They were both at the sink. Max was washing up, she was sitting on a stool with a drying cloth in her hands. He shrugged. 'Reading, writing—why?'

'If you should be working you don't have to sit around and talk to me.'

He grinned at her. 'If I should be working what makes you think I would sit around talking to you?'

'Tomorrow,' she said, 'I'll buy a notebook and some pencils, then I can be working too. And I'll get a good thick book for reading.'

'Are you bored?'

'Not in a million years, but I don't want to get in your way.'

He handed her a just washed plate and she dried it. 'Not in a million years,' he said.

But this afternoon something had not been right. Abbie could see no flaw in the way their relationship was developing, but Max expected trouble. He found her attractive, but perhaps he was afraid she might turn possessive. Maybe he was going to warn her that he didn't need a permanent crewmate.

She was glad now that he hadn't said anything, although for a while she had been desperate for an explanation. She was not possessive. She would not intrude anywhere he did not want her to be, and there must be ways of reassuring him about that without making a great issue of it.

She went fairly early to her cabin. That would give Max an hour or two before he turned in himself. He could read, or work if his mind was fresh enough for work at the end of the day. He might even miss her, which would be splendid.

When Abbie had said, 'I think I'll have an early night,' he had agreed it was a good idea.

'Are you feeling all right?' he had asked her.

'Fine,' she had said. 'But if we're off to St Ives after breakfast I might as well take my leg to bed now. I want to walk round on it tomorrow.'

The graze was healing well, although it was going to be some time before she would look her best in a swimsuit. That was a nuisance. She had shorts in her luggage, and her long slim legs were one of her best features, but this wasn't pretty, and by the time it had healed and started to fade her two weeks would be up.

She didn't mean it. She didn't believe that at all. She sat in her little cabin and knew that Max would take her to St Columb's at the end of next week, and maybe sail away. But not without telling her when he would be back and fixing their next meeting. There was no question of time being up for them. This was the beginning of the best of their lives.

The night was stifling hot again, but she didn't go up on deck. She changed to the bunk under the porthole, and stripped off, and tried to 'think cool'. Surprisingly she slept well, and when Max knocked on the door with 'Tea up!' she croaked,

'Hold on a minute!' frantically reaching for her kimono.

She opened the door and her mug of tea was outside.

'Thank you,' she called in the direction that Max had gone. 'Tomorrow I'll get up first.'.

They had breakfast and upped anchors and sailed across the Irish Sea until they reached the harbour of St Ives.

The first thing Abbie did there was buy a postcard for Maudie which she wrote in the post office. 'I'm sailing with Max Routlege. I'll be home on Friday the 12th. Marvellous boat, marvellous weather, exactly the holiday I needed. Love to you and Ben. Hope the builders came.'

'Nobody else?' said Max, as she bought a single stamp.

'No.' She couldn't think of anyone else who needed to be reassured that she was all right. She said, 'I'll wait till I get back before I tell my father where I've been. I was supposed to be keeping an eye on some building alterations in his study. Maudie knows exactly what has to be done, but if he finds I'm not around he might feel rather let down.'

'I'm sure he might,' said Max laconically. 'Aren't you writing to Bryan Gibson?'

'Why should I?'

'You might be telling him the cold fish has found other fish in the sea.'

She dropped Maudie's card into the 'Letters' slit and walked out of the post office, getting caught in a family group and almost falling over a low pushchair. Max took her arm, and walked out with her, his hand cupping her elbow, while she tried to decide if she was annoyed or not.

She might have written to Bryan. If she had done it would have been to pay him out for what she had overheard him saying about her. That would be a human enough reaction and serve him right, but he wasn't worth the bother.

She asked, 'Do you think I'm a cold fish?' but when

Max smiled her lips curved too, and she widened her smile into a grimace at him.

'Is that what Anne was doing?' she asked. 'Using you to make one of her ex-husbands jealous?'

'Very likely.'

'Didn't you mind?'

'In that case, no. But in your case the answer would be yes, I should mind.'

She could have thrown her arms around him and kissed him. It was so incredible that Max should be even the slightest degree jealous of Bryan. She said, 'Well, I'm not sending him a postcard because I have nothing to say to him. Now I remember, I never did, and all he ever said to me that made real sense was when he asked me if my father could get him a job in filming.'

'Would he have done?' Max asked.

'No. Bryan didn't know, of course, but the last night my father was in England we were talking about him, and my father said that Bryan was a lightweight who would never amount to much because he didn't have a mind of his own.'

'Shrewd judge,' said Max. 'Do you want to do any shopping?'

Abbie did. She got herself a notebook and a cartridge pen with a couple of refills. She was going to keep a diary, jotting down anything she might want to read again later about the island. She bought a couple of paperback romances for late night reading, a small bottle of a cheap and cheerful new perfume, and a long skirt in Indian cotton, patterned in mauves and purples and smoky reds. With the skirt she got a pair of hoop earrings.

For the gipsy in her soul? Max inquired, and she laughed at him. 'With my colouring? When did you last see a blonde gipsy?'

They ate at a pub on the waterfront, drinking iced

lager, and selecting from a long wide counter of sea-food. Neither of their faces was that familiar to the public, but the *Cormorant* could be recognised by someone in one of the other boats. If they were seen together tongues would start wagging, and after lunch when Max suggested, 'Shall we go?' Abbie was quick to agree.

'Anywhere else?' he asked, as the engines took them out into the open sea. 'Do you want to call in on St Columb's?'

She stood beside him at the wheel and shook her head emphatically. 'I want to go straight back to the island.'

Last time they had been en route to the island she had kept out of his way, but this afternoon she had no cause to hide. He let her take the wheel, and she thought it would be thrilling to handle a boat as he did, holding it on a tricky course, keeping it from the rocks, catching the wind in the white billowing sails as a bird uses its wings.

Watching her obvious delight he said, 'I wonder you've never had a boat, living on the coast.'

'My father doesn't like——' she began. Then, after a moment, she smiled. 'No,' she said, 'somehow we never did.'

When they neared the island Max took over, of course; he wasn't likely to trust her steering anywhere near those rocks. They came quietly into the cove, and she watched the chain cables unravelling into the green water as the anchors went down.

We're home, she thought. Safely home.

She had brought a pebble back with her, picked up from the beach at St Ives. It was a yellowish stone that she hoped would polish into a fascimile of amber. She put it with the other two, in a nest of white tissue on the dressing-table ledge in her cabin.

When she looked at it she would remember the day

Max had been jealous of Bryan, and told her that he hadn't minded Anne using him to bring back another man, but that he would care if Abbie did.

On yesterday's stone he had said that she couldn't bore him in a million years, so how many more before she could say, 'He kissed me that day ... he said things that were sweet to hear?' Would there be a stone that she would never look at without remembering ... that day he loved me?

The meal was easy enough tonight. They had bought steak on the mainland and Max cooked it. When Abbie came into the saloon it was ready.

She was wearing her white cheesecloth blouse—she had washed it last night and left it on deck this morning to dry—and her new long skirt and her new hoop earrings, and Max said, 'You look quite a girl.'

'That's how I smell too.' She had dabbed the perfume liberally on every pulse point she knew, and now she went up to him and held her hand in front of his face, wrist towards him, asking, 'Do you like it?'

She had been stuck with one brand of perfume since she was seventeen. Her father always bought it for her, and so did friends from time to time. Everyone knew Abigail Lansing's favourite perfume and nobody ever asked if she fancied a change.

The publicity blurb that advertised the scent she had bought today sounded more like Abbie than Abigail. It cost a fraction of the price of her regular perfume, and when she'd tried out the tester she had liked it.

This was the first full scale blast Max had got of it. He breathed in and blinked. 'Interesting,' he said. 'I'll find you in the dark with that on.'

'Maybe I've overdone it.' She sniffed again, herself. 'Never mind.' She blew on her wrist. 'It's bound to evaporate. Or we could always eat on deck if I'm too overpowering close to.'

He laughed. 'Shall we take the food up? Nothing to do with your aroma, of course.'

She wondered now why they hadn't done that before. 'Do let's,' she said.

She sat on the chair she had slept in the night before last, and Max sat on the deck. They balanced plates on their knees, with condiments, glasses, bread and fruit scattered around them. They were in time for a glorious sunset, and everything was nearly perfect.

'Max,' said Abbie, when the main meal was over and the sunset had faded into pinks and greys, 'who is the girl I remind you of?'

He held his wineglass in his right hand, an apple in his left. He finished the mouthful of apple he was biting into and then asked, 'What girl?'

Perhaps he didn't want to discuss those memories, but after so direct a question she had to explain herself. 'When I asked you what you'd got against me you said you had some memories. But we'd never met before, so it had to be a girl who seemed like me. Didn't it? You certainly had it in for somebody.'

He threw his apple core over the side with a plop. 'We all have our prejudices,' he said cheerfully. 'Mine was a general one. I'm allergic to the type you seemed to be.'

'Oh!' She would rather he had not cared deeply enough for another girl to feel bitter about her still, although it had seemed like personal antagonism to Abbie. She supposed she believed him, but she wasn't sure. She said lightly, 'If you brought me here to study my reaction to the spartan life shall you write about me?'

His voice was teasing and affectionate. 'Ah, but I didn't realise who I was bringing. I didn't know Abbie then.'

'You won't write about Abbie?'

117

A shadow fell across his face, shuttering it, so that it was as though a window closed. She couldn't read his eyes and his mouth was straight and unsmiling, although he still sounded as though he was teasing her. 'Time will tell,' he said.

He meant he might, but he didn't know what. He was not so sure that the story of Abbie would be a happy one. She took a peach from the bowl of fruit. It was sweet, she knew, but the trickle of juice tasted sour on her tongue.

'Anyhow,' she said, 'I won't be in your next book?'

'I promise you that.'

'Will you keep me for your old age? The chapter on girls I have known?' She didn't want him to answer, she daren't look at him. She went on quickly, 'What *is* your next book or play going to be about?' and to her surprise he told her.

She was caught at once. Even if it hadn't been Max's brainchild she would still have found it an enthralling theme. He ran through the plot, without wasting words, in a kind of verbal shorthand, but it was going to be riveting and the final dramatic twist had her gasping, eyes wide and mouth open.

She went on gasping until he tipped her chin, with a fingertip, closing her mouth. Then she gulped, 'I don't believe it. But that is exactly what could happen. I can't wait to read it.'

'You're the sort of audience I like,' he said. 'Now finish your peach.' She was holding that in front of her, and she looked down at it, still slightly disorientated.

'You are so clever,' she said, and she meant it and nobody could deny it. Max didn't. He grinned and said,

'Yes, I know. And what about you? You're a smart girl. With both parents such stars didn't you ever consider an acting career?'

'Oh yes, when I was fifteen I wanted to go to drama

school, but my father told me I didn't have the talent to follow in their footsteps, and the critics would have had a field day with anything less, wouldn't they?'

Max didn't answer. She went on, 'He was right, of course. If I'd had the makings of a star quality actress I wouldn't have given up the idea that easily.'

But her father's word had always been her ultimate ruling on everything. One sign of encouragement from him when she was fifteen could have changed her life. She put that thought away from her and Max said, 'About your writing.'

'My celebrity spots? Pathetic.' She gave a deep mock sigh of self-disgust. 'On Friday we could sail in and pick up a paper and you could see what I said about you. Then you'd understand why Hugh thought I might have got something a bit livelier.'

'You're not afraid of them any more,' said Max, 'so the next spot should be livelier.'

'Would you mind——?' He knew what was coming. She spoke cajolingly. 'Please would you mind if I wrote an article for the *Telegraph* about here?'

'So long as you don't turn it into a tourist spot. I need space sometimes. It comes of being institutionalised at an early age.'

'I wouldn't say where it was exactly,' she promised eagerly. 'And there's a lot of sea around, it shouldn't get overrun.'

Max agreed. 'All right, you write what you like.'

'About you?'

'Sure, why not? Start off with me for the livelier Celebrity Spot.' He raised his glass. 'Here's to Abbie Lansing, columnist, uncensored and unafraid.'

'I'll drink to that.' But she bit into her peach instead and said mischievously, 'Actually, after I wrote the copy on you that I handed in I did a spoof article to amuse myself. I didn't show it to anyone, I didn't think anyone in the house would appreciate it, so I tore it up as soon as I finished it, but I was wishing I'd had the nerve to ask you some real questions over that dinner table.'

They were both remembering the scene that night, King Leo holding court, his daughter for the most part silent, and under the smiling socialising the undertow of antagonism between Max Routlege and Abigail Lansing.

'You were the first guest I wanted to put on the spot,' said Abbie, 'because you were putting me on the spot.'

They both smiled at the idiocy of those first impressions. How wrong could you get? 'I'd have liked to see the article you tore up,' Max chuckled.

'I wonder I didn't make a mistake and hand it in instead of the genuine article,' said Abbie with dancing eyes. 'I wonder my subconscious didn't fix it, the way I was seething under the skin. And it's always possible Hugh might have printed it. What would you have done then? Sued the *Penrann Telegraph*?'

Max entered into the joke. 'Not unless you said I'm paying someone else to ghost my work.'

'No, I don't remember saying that.'

'Practically everything else has been said, some time or other.'

'It has, hasn't it?' She was surprised how much she could remember of the things that had been written about Max Routlege, considering he hadn't even met him when she'd read them. Her mind flicked over newspaper reports of hair-raising adventures. The men whose company he kept always seemed to have brains and courage, the women always seemed to be intelligent and attractive.

She said, 'What the papers write about you is more interesting than what they write about me. I'm the girl only a father could love.'

She could say that smiling, because it was never going to be true again. 'Rubbish,' said Max.

'Thank you, but when they said, "Another romance

has gone sour on Abigail Lansing," what they meant was—another man has walked out on her.'

Max raised an incredulous eyebrow. 'No!'

'Yes.' She was gratified he was finding it incredible. He disliked the type of girl he had believed Abigail Lansing to be, but he couldn't believe that she had been jilted time and again.

Not that she had been jilted. Nothing so dramatic. She said, 'There were no big scenes. After a while they just sort of drifted off. Some sooner, some later.' She laughed. 'That sounds like a procession, doesn't it? There were four altogether. Four in five years isn't so many, is it? And that includes Bryan.'

'And the four of them "just sort of drifted off"?' His eyes were narrowed now, watching her closely. 'Why?'

'They didn't say why. Well, Bryan didn't drift, but he would have done as soon as he realised I couldn't help him get that job, and the novelty of being seen around with King Leo's daughter wore off.' She could say it all without rancour, as though they were discussing another girl with whom she had little in common. She could understand it, and even find it wryly amusing.

'I don't understand it,' said Max.

'I do,' said Abbie. 'They thought that Abigail Lansing had to be fantastic, with the mother and father she had, and Abigail Lansing was not fantastic.' She had finished her peach. She held the stone in her hand and thought what a pretty shape it was, like an intricate carving. She wondered someone hadn't sold one to the Tate. She smiled up at Max. 'You remember Abigail?' she said. 'She was nothing.'

That was what he had said himself. That should have made him smile, but it didn't. 'You let them go without asking for an explanation?' he said.

'What else could I do?' He couldn't be jealous of such an empty past, nor was it even interesting. Maybe this was the writer, curious about everything. He didn't suggest what she might have done. He just sat there, waiting for her to say something else. 'None of them mattered,' she said.

Except Stephen. Stephen had mattered most, but when she looked at Max now she knew how little that had been. 'I cried for one,' she said, 'that was all.'

If he had said, 'Who was that?' she would have told him, but again he said nothing.

'Have you ever cried for a woman?' she asked, lightly because of course he hadn't.

'Not yet,' he said. Not ever, she thought. She said, 'I don't recommend it. It isn't much fun.'

'I can imagine.' Then he asked abruptly, 'What did your father have to say about them all?'

Her expression became tender. 'Oh, he was marvellous. They weren't even affairs, you know, they were just men who seemed to be fond of me and took me around and then lost interest, but my father wouldn't let me feel badly about them. He knew they weren't the right one, he always said so afterwards.' But he couldn't say that about Max. He would be happy for her and Max.

She said gaily, 'You know, he even bought me consolation prizes. Jewellery usually. After Stephen he took me to Paris for two weeks and bought me dresses. Wasn't that crazy? But it was kind, wasn't it?'

'It seems the least he could do,' Max muttered.

'What?' Abbie couldn't think what he meant by that.

'More wine?' he asked.

'No, thanks. What did you just say?'

'Nothing.' He wasn't repeating it. He poured another half glass for himself and began to describe the vineyard in Corbière from which the wine had come, and perhaps she had misheard what she thought he had said ...

Next day Max finished the upstairs flooring of the cottage, and Abbie started the downstairs painting.

They walked along the beach and across the plain, across the stream.

'I want to climb the peaks,' Abbie said.

'We will,' Max promised, 'but not today.'

The peaks were high and her leg was stiff, and there were still a lot of tomorrows. But there seemed to be fewer hours in these days, and suddenly a week was over.

There was the cottage to show for that week. You could have lived in it now, quite comfortably. Max had ferried things round, that he had brought in the *Cormorant* to leave in the cottage. He had cleaned out the chimney and they had lit a fire and boiled a kettle.

Abbie hadn't tried cooking in the oven. That would have been very hit-or-miss, and in any case they always went back to the boat at night where the galley oven had a thermostat and two gas burners.

Sleeping arrangements and toilet facilities were better on the boat. There was still only one camp bed in the cottage, and no bedding at all. But one morning, while they were having breakfast, Abbie said, 'How about taking along the sleeping bags and a couple of lamps and staying in the cottage tonight?'

'I don't think so,' said Max.

'Why not?' She *wanted* to stay in the cottage. It was as though she had helped build it and owned a stake in it. She wanted to see it by night as well as day.

'This is more convenient,' said Max.

Her cabin was snug and compact, with its separate toilet compartment of course it was convenient. But there was running water and a chemical loo at the cottage. 'I don't mind roughing it a little,' she said.

'No,' said Max.

'All right, I'll camp out myself.'

'Please yourself,' he said.

But she didn't. She took her sleeping bag along with her in the dinghy, but when Max went back to the

Cormorant she went too. 'It's your turn to cook to-night,' she said. 'I've decided to camp out on a night when it's mine.'

She had a pebble for every day, and some very attractive shells; but there wasn't a pebble for the day Max first kissed her, still less for the day he told her he loved her. Because he hadn't yet.

They got on splendidly. Everything they did together was like the pebbles would be when they were polished, bright and lovely. Eating, talking, working, walking. Everything. But he hadn't kissed her.

She wished he would. She longed to be drawn into his arms, to feel his mouth on hers, but she was afraid to be the one who did the reaching in the first place. She didn't know how to make a first move that wouldn't be gauche and awkward.

Perhaps she shouldn't have told Max how inexperienced she was. She should have let him think that at least one of the men who had drifted out of her life had been her lover. A first time was more likely to be a commitment, and perhaps he wasn't ready to commit himself.

And yet Abbie was within a hair's breadth of certainty that he loved her. She saw it sometimes in the way he looked at her, she heard it in the caress of his voice. He was tough and experienced and cynical, and if she was no more to him than any other attractive willing girl surely he would have made casual love to her before now.

Her feelings were not casual in any way, and there was no reason why they shouldn't spend the night in the cottage, except that it was a little house and the door between the rooms upstairs didn't fit too well. On the *Cormorant* at night the doors shut perfectly and since that first night Abbie had stayed in her cabin, not venturing up on deck, and that was how Max seemed to want it.

He wasn't rushing things, and she told herself that she didn't mind. This was her first real friendship, out of her father's shadow, and she knew it was going to be her first real love and her last. It was still less than a month since she and Max had met. She was sure that soon he would tell her he loved her, deeply and lastingly.

Max was pointing the outside walls of the cottage these days, and Abbie was helping. But as they brought the dinghy in to Seal Sands that morning he said, 'What about taking the day off?'

'And why not? We've earned it,' she said happily.

She had started swimming again, this side of the island. The graze on her leg was still unsightly. She had hesitated about displaying it. 'It's ugly,' she'd protested, but Max had laughed.

'Fishing for compliments? All right—nothing about you could be ugly. Now, I'm going in. What are you going to do, paddle?'

They had swum together every day after that, and a whole day of swimming and loafing would have been enjoyable, but when he asked now, 'Do you think you could manage to get up one of the peaks?' that was a better idea.

'Of course I could,' she said promptly.

'It's a fair climb—you can see that. And there isn't much to choose between them.'

'I've been clambering up and down the cliff by Players' Court since I can't remember when,' she told him, and he laughed.

'I've seen you. I was rowing back to the boat and I watched you going up like a small white goat. At the top you turned and made a very impertinent gesture.'

'I wouldn't know an impertinent gesture if I saw one,' she grinned. 'I was reared to be a lady, I'll have you remember, and that was a ladylike wave.'

'Not from where I was rowing,' he said. 'But you

know how to climb your cliff, so I should think you can get up mine.'

Climbing mountains was one of his hobbies. He had set a couple of TV plays in high, white, perilous places, so Abbie wasn't likely to slip if he was beside her. Especially as he tied a thin length of strong nylon rope around her waist, ending round his.

'If you go, I go,' she said. She knew he wouldn't fall, she was joking, and he smiled at her.

'That's a risk you'll have to take.'

That's how I'd want it to be, she thought. If you go there is nothing left in all the world for me. She laughed and said, 'I always knew you were a bully.'

Both peaks rose sharply from the plain, looking almost sheer. At the beginning, on the west peak, they found footholds in the tough springy dark grass. Tiny flowers dotted here and there, some with minute blue or white bell-petals, some like miniature red daisies.

'Pretty,' said Abbie. 'What are they called?'

'I wouldn't know,' said Max.

'I'll find out.' She picked specimens, slipping them into the breast pocket of her shirt, although it didn't matter what label they had. They were the flowers of the western peak, and they were beautiful.

About half way up the vegetation petered into sparse moss, picked out occasionally still by the tiny patches of colour, and Abbie found that she was having to pull herself up. Sometimes when she grasped a jutting piece the mossy covering would peel off in her hands. Now and then, through the rocks, she caught the glimpse of water that was trickling down to the stream below.

It was hard going. She was perspiring and so was Max. He was just ahead of her, and when he turned she saw his face glistening. She copied every move and handhold he made, and kept the nylon cord slack between them.

When he stopped so did she, looking down with a

gasp at how far below the plain seemed to be. 'Don't look down!' Max called.

That was a stupid thing to do, she had looked without thinking. It was different on the cliffs around her home. She knew them so well. This wasn't more than sixty or seventy feet, and it wasn't a sheer fall, but the rocks sticking out looked jagged and menacing.

'All right?' Max was asking.

'Fine.' Her voice was a trifle high-pitched.

'Move your left hand to that rock above you, and feel with your right foot for a crack in the rocks. It's there for you.' He was calm and quiet and confident, and if she had been frozen with sudden panic she knew that his voice would have been a lifeline.

I love you, she thought. Oh, I was blessed in meeting you.

From above Max sounded irascible. 'Come *on*, for godsake! How long do you expect me to wait around here?' He thought she *had* panicked. He was deliberately goading her, to jerk her out of her immobility, and she looked up at him and grimaced.

'Shut up,' she said sweetly. 'I'm only getting my breath.' As he burst out laughing she said, 'I'm rested. You may proceed.'

At the top he reached out a hand to pull her the last few feet, and she scrambled up beside him. 'I thought you'd frozen on me,' he said.

'Never.' She could promise that, and he knew what she was promising. His arm around her tightened and it seemed that understanding flowed between them, but he drew her no closer, and after a moment he stopped looking at her and looked around.

So did she. They were on a flattish plateau, not very large, from which pinnacles of rock reached up skywards. On the top of one pinnacle an enormous dark bird was standing, watching them. As Abbie pointed it rose in the air screaming, its tremendous wings beating

127

slowly as it swept down the seaward side of the peak.

'Another cormorant?' asked Abbie. As splendid as their *Cormorant*, their boat. Max nodded.

'That was the sentinel bird, warning the others it's spied strangers.'

They crossed to the seaward side, and lay flat to look over the edge, down a sheer tumble of rocks. Birds were wheeling above and below them, clouds of birds.

'The cormorants are mostly in nesting holes in the rock,' Max explained softly against the screaming birds and the howling wind. 'Most of these are tern.'

'No gulls?' Abbie was curious. 'I've noticed that.'

'Any who arrive to try to steal eggs or fledglings get short shrift.'

'What's that one?' She lifted her head, following the flight, high over the sea, of a great bird poised and wheeling, its huge wings stretched out like a sail-plane as it glided. Suddenly it swooped down to the water, its wings closed as it hit the sea and vanished.

'An auk, I think,' said Max. 'There are one or two about. Can you see the seals?'

Abbie leaned over cautiously, and Max put a hand on her shoulder, checking her, so that she covered his fingers with her own and smiled at him. 'I won't stretch out too far.'

'I'm sure you won't,' he said. 'But you must admit you are accident-prone.'

'No, I'm not,' she denied it indignantly. 'One leg scrape while swimming doesn't make a casebook.'

'How about getting yourself stuck on a rock in a thunderstorm?'

'Could have happened to anybody.'

'Could it?' said Max. 'All the same, keep back from the edge. You can still see the seals.'

There was Seal Sands, way down on the left of them, and the tiny black heads in the water. Here and there a seal flopped on to a rock for a while, before waddling and sliding back into the water. It all looked great fun. 'Seals know how to enjoy themselves,' said Abbie. 'Some of my best friends are seals.'

That had become true this week. She was sure she could recognise her favourites. She was sure they knew her. She meant to be here in the spring when the cubs came.

The tern and a few cormorants still wheeled and glided uneasily just below them, aware of the peering visitors, but the birds' screaming lessened, so that the main sound was the keening wind and the slap of the waves on the rocks below.

They had a magnificent vantage point up here, but the wind was cold and Max said, 'Time to go.'

'Yes.' They had caused enough disturbance. Tonight she would write it all up in her diary. She wrote about everything she saw. Not her feelings. Just descriptions, facts, a record of her stay. She was not yet uninhibited enough to put down her emotions on paper.

They walked across the plateau, across the light sparse brittle grass, and she picked up a grey pebble on the way. After peering over the seaward cliff the landward side of the peak seemed less steep, and the going down was easier than the climbing had been.

'Why are there no birds this side?' Abbie asked, rather breathlessly, as they neared the plain.

'No food,' said Max.

At the bottom of the peak she took a deep breath, at a loss for words.

'That was—marvellous,' she said. 'It was—well, it was just fantastic. One day, please, will you take me up a mountain?'

He was undoing the cord from around his waist, and she tried to undo hers. But the unslippable knots were hard and tight, and her fingertips were sore from clinging to the rough rocks. She wouldn't mention that, they'd soon be all right.

Max took over, pulling the knots apart so that the cord slipped from her. 'Tomorrow,' she said, 'we'll work twice as hard to make up for taking today off,' and he said,

'We'll be leaving here tomorrow.'

'Oh no!' Her cry was a protest and a plea. They had another week. All along he had said that he was here for a fortnight. When they'd talked ahead they had always planned for what was left of fourteen days. '*Why?*' she demanded.

'I've some business to attend to,' Max said, and for the first time since that first day here she faced the possibility that he was getting out of her life. There was no future for them. He had seen the danger signs and he was taking her home.

She had thought she would fight for Max, but what could she do if he sailed away and left her on the quayside of St Columb's Cove?

What business could he have? There were no phones here, no mail. Whatever it was had come out of his own mind, and what reason could there be for leaving, except that he had decided against staying any longer? She said in the cool level voice she had used when she first met him, 'I've heard that before. "I've some business to attend to." That's what Stephen told me before he went, and I never saw nor heard of him again.'

She began to walk away, and when Max said, 'Abbie,' she walked faster. Maybe he was going to tell her it wasn't like that at all. That he'd planned to take a fortnight to put the cottage to rights, but there had been two of them so the work was halved—well, nearly halved—and of course he wanted to get down to the book, but when they got back he wasn't going to let her out of his sight.

Please let it be that simple and that miraculous. But she went on walking, almost running, because she couldn't believe her dream. If Max was taking her home because the idyll was over he would let her go now, and hope that her pride and her common sense would take over.

If it wasn't that he would follow her and tell her what it was. If he ran after her and caught her she would be in his arms, and then he *couldn't* say, 'Goodbye, Abbie.'

'*Abbie!*' He was following her, and she ran now because the tears were blinding her, and she couldn't face him, trying to blink them away before he reached her. Whatever he said she mustn't be weeping.

She neither looked nor cared where she was running. She went blundering through the bracken and fern, and as Max called her name again her feet came down on nothing, and she screeched and dropped into the hole of a 'chimney'.

It was deep enough down to squash the breath out of her, like falling from that tree when she was a child. Then the sky had swirled and shimmered above, now it was a hole over her head.

Then Max's face appeared in it, and if she had had breath to say anything she might have said, 'Hi, man in the moon,' because the shock had knocked her silly. She was going to start giggling if she didn't get a tight hold on herself.

'Are you all right?' Max was shouting.

She gulped in enough breath to say, 'Fine.'

She wasn't stuck. This chimney went almost straight for about seven feet, then it began to slope downwards. It was dark, although Max was tearing away the bracken above. 'I can get out,' she said, and she did giggle in nervous reaction.

'Then get out!' Max shouted.

If Abbie had been alone her instinct for survival would have had her clawing her way to the surface, but not immediately because her legs felt rubbery. She stood up and they buckled beneath her, as she sagged against the rocky sides of the tunnel.

'Wait a bit,' she croaked. 'When's high tide likely to be coming up here?'

'Around November,' said Max. 'Stay where you are.'

He sounded much as he had on the mountainside, when he'd thought she was panicking. But he wasn't trying to anger her into forgetting her peril now because she was in no peril, so he must be genuinely annoyed.

He had said she was accident-prone. She never had been, but maybe it was one of Abbie's traits, and perhaps it was getting a bit much.

He was back in no time, lowering the nylon rope down to her, ordering her, 'Tie that round your waist. Do you know how?'

'Yes,' she said, and secured herself to the end, wincing at the smart of her skinned fingertips.

Then he yanked her up and she 'walked' the side of the chimney until she was head and shoulders out of the hole, gripping the edges, being gripped by Max and unceremoniously hauled out.

She got off her knees and said, 'If I'd got until next November what was the rush?'

'It was not funny.' He *was* angry. He gave her a couple of brisk shakes and she said furiously,

'I wasn't playing the fool, I couldn't help it. It wasn't my fault there was a gaping great hole in the ground. I'd have got out, you needn't have bothered about me.'

He was still gripping her. 'Oh God,' he said huskily, 'I didn't know how deep it was. I didn't know how I was going to get you out.'

He wrapped his arms around her, and looked at her upturned face with an agonised longing. As his mouth closed on hers, every nerve in her dissolved. She clung to him, needing him so much it was terrifying. Her heart was pounding and when her lips were free she whispered, 'Oh, I love you so.'

That was all he had to say to keep her in his arms.

But he said nothing, and he wasn't holding her any longer. His hands were loose by his sides. She stood alone, bewildered, waiting to be told why his arms were no longer around her.

CHAPTER SEVEN

'I LOVE you,' Abbie said again. This time she didn't whisper it as she had just done, dreamily and happily. She said it in a thin voice that sounded scared. Because she was scared. She was remembering the others who had gone away, and she knew that if Max went she would learn what black loneliness meant.

Then he said, 'I'm glad about that,' and she breathed again. If he was glad it had to mean he loved her. But if he loved her why was he standing away from her now?

'Then why——?' she stammered. She held her hands towards him and when he made no move she pressed both hands to her mouth, her grave eyes questioning and beseeching.

'And why are we leaving here tomorrow?' he said.

Of course she wanted that explained. It was all one, that and this. 'I'll tell you why,' he said quietly. 'Because if I take you I'm not handing you back to any-one. It would be for ever.'

That sank in slowly. She was so sure she was going to be hurt that, although she'd heard what he was saying, she couldn't believe it meant—I could love you for the rest of my life.

She stared at him and there was no arrogance in him now. Determination still, the mouth was set, but his eyes were almost afraid, and then she realised what he had just said and she was radiant with joy.

'Yes,' she said. She put her arms around him, inter-twining her fingers behind his head. 'For ever,' she said. 'Yes.'

'I want you to be sure.' His hands were on her shoulders. She tried to pull down his face so that her lips could reach his, but she couldn't. 'And this is no way, no place,' he said.

'This is our magic island,' she reminded him.

'Exactly.' He smiled wryly, 'You might find the spell breaks when you get back to Players' Court.'

A tiny doubt reached her, just enough to make her unlock her fingers from behind his head and ask, 'Do you mean that you might?'

'I don't think so.'

'But we'd better both wait and see?'

'You could put it like that.'

She could think of a reason. 'Do I have a rival?' Not Anne, he had said, but Anne was a long way from being his only female friend. Perhaps there was someone else he might be comparing Abbie with when they returned to the temperate climate of the workaday world.

'You don't,' he said, and her heart soared at that. 'But I may have.'

Bryan? Max couldn't imagine she'd look at Bryan again. She began to smile and asked, 'Do you love me?'

'Yes.'

That was all that mattered. Now she could face anything. She could sail away from here tomorrow and know they would come back. She laughed very softly. 'That, my darling,' she said, 'seems to be all that matters to me, but all right, we'll do it your way. We'll go back —I don't have much choice, do I?—and then I'll tell you again that I love you, each hour of every day if you like.'

'Just don't tell me now.' He brushed back her hair tenderly from her face and smiled down at her. 'But this time next week and I warn you——'

It was a powerful physical attraction they had for each other, and more. Abbie knew that his lovemaking would take her by storm and flood to paradise, but he was already her best friend in the world.

She said, 'So I'm warned. This time next week? I'll keep that in mind.'

'This time next week.' He spoke lightly as though they were making a casual date. Then he said, 'If you want to marry me then you can tell me when.'

'Couldn't I say now? This day next month I'll marry you, that gives me plenty of time. Couldn't I say that?'

They still smiled. It couldn't really matter if Max wouldn't let her promise anything until she was back at Players' Court. She wasn't infatuated, she loved him, and in a week's time she'd say, 'Let's get married in three weeks,' so it would still only be a month.

Max was shaking his head, and she said, 'No? I can't say that?'

'No.'

'Then please will you turn up in a week wherever I am, and ask me to marry you? I'd like that. Nobody ever has.'

She sobered as she said it, because she was so glad nobody ever had. She might have said yes and taken someone else, when Max was the man for whom every cell in her body and brain hungered.

'I'll be there,' he said.

'Bring the ring,' she told him gaily. 'Nothing flashy. I've got too much of the flashy stuff. I'd really like a polished pebble, but failing that——' The curious shuttered shadow was on his face again and it stopped her teasing prattle. She hadn't really been teasing. This was serious, wasn't it?

She said slowly, 'Max, we're not playing games, are we?'

He looked grimmer than she had ever seen him. Briefly, for a moment, he looked harder than granite. 'This is no game,' he said, and that was all the reassurance she needed, and there was no cause for grimness, goodness knows, because no one was going to be hurt.

'Right,' said Max. 'Let's get back to the *Cormorant*.'

'Seeing that it's our last night, why don't we stay in the cottage?' As he hesitated she pressed on, 'We've done all this work on it, and I want to sleep in it for one night.' She added mischievously, 'I can have downstairs and you can have upstairs if you talk in your sleep and you don't want me overhearing you.'

'For other reasons the sleeping accommodation would be well apart,' he said. 'And I don't talk in my sleep.' He grinned. 'At least I've never been told I do.'

'Pity.' They were arm in arm now, making their way to Seal Sands and the dinghy. 'I might have learned about your disreputable past.'

'You'll hear about that all right,' he said cheerfully.

'Awful, was it?'

'I enjoyed most of it very much, thank you.'

'I hope you enjoy your future.' I need you, I will make you happy, she was telling him, and his hand tightened on her arm, holding her closer.

'So long as it's our future,' he said, 'it will be quite a life.'

Abbie was sure of it. She was almost anxious now for morning to come and for them to set sail back to St Columb's Cove, if that was the way to convince Max that he was the man who mattered in her life. There *was* something spellbinding about this island, but the feelings that this week had evoked had little to do with surroundings. Learning to know Max Routlege she had found understanding and true companionship, and a passion in herself she had never suspected. There was passion in him too, a restrained passion that stirred her tenderness as well as her love.

They had never been closer than they were that evening. They had never spoken of love until today and now, for Abbie at least, the future was sure and shining.

They brought sleeping bags from the *Cormorant* and

left them, rolled up, in the corner of the living room, while they ate their evening meal and talked by lamp-light.

Max had a flat in Richmond, overlooking the Thames. He described it for her, and although it would be her home as well there was a tacit understanding between them that neither said that in so many words.

Marriage wasn't mentioned again. In a week's time, before that probably, it would be, but tonight they were lovers only in the looks they exchanged. Not by touch, not by word. Just free-as-air friends. Committed till death and beyond, thought Abbie, and smiled at Max and almost said, 'Next time we come here we shall be husband and wife.'

Around midnight, when she was yawning and trying to hide it, Max said, 'Time for bed.'

She fluttered her eyelashes in theatrical fashion at him. 'Is that an offer?' and he laughed.

'No, it is not. You take the camp bed, I'll stay down here.'

'You're not scared of little me?'

'Too damn right I am,' he said. 'Now, are you going up or are you dossing down on the flagstones?'

She wondered if he would kiss her goodnight, or if any caress might dispel the laughter. Certainly it would be a risk, and Max was a determined man and no masochist. He had made up his mind very firmly that there was to be a breathing space, back in their usual environments, and he would do nothing to blow that decision or make it harder to carry through.

He wasn't going to kiss her. He was handing her her rolled-up sleeping bag, he wasn't going up with her either, and it would be madness for her to kiss him because he was strong-willed enough to keep it light and friendly but she could go to pieces.

She carried on fooling, asking, 'What do you think would have happened if Miranda had made the pass at Caliban, on their magic island, instead of the other way round?'

'Not a thing,' said Max promptly. 'Prospero would have seen to that.'

Miranda's father, the magician. 'Yes, of course,' said Abbie, and took her bed-roll in both arms and went up the creaking little staircase. Once through the door at the top of the stairs the talking would be over. She was unwilling to move away from the contact of his voice and she kept talking. 'My father played Prospero in the other Stratford-on-Avon, the one in Ontario, a couple of seasons ago.'

'That figures,' said Max.

Of course it did, because Leo Lansing was still a classical actor although he appeared in modern-day films and plays. 'Of course,' said Abbie, her hand on the latch of the door at the top of the stairs. She opened the door and said, 'Goodnight, love.'

'Goodnight, my love,' said Max. She wanted to look down at him. She wanted to run back to him. But she knew she must do neither, so she went through the door into the cool little room, and dropped her sleeping bag on the camp bed.

There was enough moonlight through the uncurtained window to see all she needed to see. She only had to get out of her clothes and into the sleeping bag. There would be no reading herself to sleep tonight. She had finished the first book she bought in St Ives and had expected to start the second tonight. The first book had been quite a moving love story. At least she had thought it was moving and realistic while she was reading it, but now, compared with the frightening power of her own longing, it seemed less real.

She slid down into the sleeping bag and wished tomorrow away, and the rest of the following week until Max would say, 'Marry me,' and she would say, 'Yes, for ever, yes.'

They came in to St Columb's Cove in the early afternoon, when the quayside was crowded with holiday visitors. Max wasn't going up to Players' Court, he did have some business to get out of the way which would take him about three days, and then he would be sailing back to her.

Abbie could use three days herself. There would be things to see to in her father's house. She was sure that the business excuse was genuine, but Max was giving her a break, away from him and in her old surroundings, to prove to both of them that this was no passing thing.

Of course it wasn't. She knew how deep her own feelings went, and she had no doubt about his, and three days would soon pass. Then she would come down and sit on the harbour wall and wait for him, just as she had done at their first meeting.

He put her ashore now, and she climbed up the steps, her kitbag over her shoulder, while he sat in the dinghy, hands on the oars. 'See you,' she said.

'That you will,' he told her.

She didn't stand and watch him row back to the *Cormorant*, because although she would see him again, and soon, she didn't want to watch him go, getting smaller and farther away. They hadn't said goodbye, as though that made it less of a parting, and she turned and walked quickly, not looking back at all.

Most of the crowds were holidaymakers, but she passed a few familiar faces and exchanged smiles. She was anxious now to get to the house, make sure all was well with Maudie and ponder on how she was going to let her father know what was happening. Her mind was full of that, so that she hurried on, although several people tried to keep her talking.

'Hello, had a nice trip?' was the recurring question. The way she was dressed, and carrying her kit, obviously she was returning from a spell on a boat.

'Lovely,' she told them all, as she went striding on.

Near the top of the hill Mrs Meyers, who ran a guest-house called High Tor and loved a gossip, stepped out of her entrance porch as Abbie approached on the narrow pavement. 'Good morning,' said Mrs Meyers, her plump good-humoured face fairly twinkling. 'Had a nice trip?'

'Yes, thank you,' said Abbie. 'Everything all right with you?' She would have to step off the pavement to get round Mrs Meyers, and a loaded coach was climbing slowly, filling the roadway. So she stood, waiting.

'Can't complain,' said Mrs Meyers, who rarely did. Then she twinkled again. 'Lovely boat, the *Cormorant*.'

'Oh *yes*,' said Abbie, realising this meant that everyone knew where she had been for the past week. Not about the island, but about the *Cormorant*. That was why the smiles had been so broad; everyone thought it was nice that Abigail Lansing was sea-dating Max Routlege.

She shouldn't have been surprised. Someone had probably watched her paddling out to the *Cormorant* a week ago, then bringing back the inflatable dinghy and Max collecting her. Or they could have been spotted in St Ives. Or the postcard she had sent to Maudie could have been read before it was delivered. Why not? If you wrote anything that was strictly private you should put it in an envelope.

Well, they all seemed to approve, thought Abbie, as she took the clifftop path, and Maudie certainly should. Maudie had been on Max's side from the beginning, when Abbie had thought he was unbearable. Considering how little Maudie could know of Max that had been surprising. Even with Stephen the height of Maudie's praise had been, 'He's all right, I dare say.'

The builders were in at Players' Court. Their van

stood near a back door, and when Abbie went into the house she sniffed the gritty smell of brick dust. Maudie must have seen her through a window, because she was there before Abbie had time to call out.

Abbie went into her arms, and Maudie hugged her as she had rarely done since Abbie was a child. 'I told you you needed a holiday, chicken,' Maudie chuckled.

'And you were right,' said Abbie.

'When are we seeing this friend of yours, then?' Maudie had hoped that Max Routlege would come back to Players' Court with Abbie. As he hadn't she expected Abbie to tell her he would be along later. When Abbie said,

'In about three days' time,' Maudie's, 'Oh!' sounded like a sigh.

'Anything wrong with that?' Abbie asked.

'Not as I know of,' said Maudie.

'This one will be coming back,' said Abbie. Maudie knew about the others. 'This one,' said Abbie, 'I am going to marry.'

Maudie looked almost happy again. 'Does he know that?'

'He certainly does.' Abbie had a confidence about her that Maudie had never seen before. She was glowing with health and happiness. She teased, 'He's got some business to attend to. He'll be away for three days, and then he'll come back here and tell you how honourable his intentions are, so don't you start worrying about that.'

'When's he telling your father?' Maudie demanded.

'Very soon,' said Abbie. 'Although I'll be breaking the news to my father first.'

'You won't,' said Maudie. 'Haven't you seen the papers?'

Abbie's smile was wiped clean off her face. She hadn't minded friends and neighbours knowing she had been sailing with Max. She had wanted Maudie and Ben to know that this was a love affair, that she and Max were planning marriage, but she shrank from the thought of press publicity at this stage.

She followed Maudie into the kitchen and Maudie produced a newspaper, open at the gossip page.

It was a page on which Abbie had featured before. There were separate head-and-shoulder photographs of herself and Max, under the headline, 'Abigail and Max Afloat Together.' There was a little about her, rather more about Max, and then, 'Abigail's father, actor Leo Lansing, at present filming in France, told me, "My daughter has plenty of friends. I wouldn't describe this as a romantic attachment. I don't know where they are, and I don't know who else is with them."'

'Oh dear!' muttered Abbie. 'I suppose it had to happen, but I do wish we could have taken our own time about making announcements.'

'Your father phoned through,' said Maudie. 'He wanted to know where you'd gone and when you'd be back. I told him you said next Friday—you're back early, aren't you?'

'How did he sound?' Abbie asked anxiously. 'Is he all right?'

Leo had snapped Maudie's head off, and she said with disapproval, 'Very bad-tempered.'

Abbie couldn't think why. He had never objected to her going sailing before, if he wasn't around and she wasn't needed at Players' Court; but he did like to have all the answers when reporters started questioning him. She said, 'I should have let him know where I was, but it wasn't that easy, although I could have written when I sent your card.'

'But you didn't,' said Maudie.

'No.' Abbie took another look at the photograph of Max. She seemed to remember it and she wondered what story it had accompanied last time. This gossip snippet was a nuisance, but she wanted the small column-wide photograph of Max.

She said, 'I think I'll write to my father. I can talk better on paper than I could over the telephone, and there's so much I have to tell him.'

She was smiling again now, and Maudie ached for her, knowing that Leo Lansing would never surrender Abbie willingly, even if it meant breaking her heart. She warned, 'Don't expect an easy time with your father.'

Abbie gave a thoughtful little nod. 'Yes, I do see that he's going to think this all very sudden, so we'll have to convince him it's the real thing, won't we? When he understands that will be all right.' Her face lit up, translucent with happiness, and she said softly, 'Of course he'll understand. He's always been the best father in the world.'

The first and only time Maudie saw Max Routlege she had thought he looked tough enough to take on Leo Lansing. She was glad he wanted to marry Abbie, but she knew that the immediate future must bring bitterness.

Abbie went singing around the house. She looked in on the builders. They were getting along well and were pleased to see her. She looked a girl who would brighten anyone's day.

Then she went through the mail, taking the letters that were for her up to the bedroom, grimacing at two notes from Bryan, unpacking, having a quick bath and getting into clean clothes.

She tore up Bryan's notes and arranged her collection of shells and pebbles on her dressing table. When Max came back he would get that bracelet made for her. Until then she could look at the pebbles as they were, and remember.

The phone rang several times that day. Friends who had read that the columnist suspected romance rang to see if Abigail was home again. When they got Abbie

144

they asked her and she said, 'We've only known each other a few days,' and because Abigail Lansing had seemed the last girl for a whirlwind romance they thought that was an answer.

Hugh Trelawney rang from the *Penrann Telegraph* and said, 'You're a dark horse—you never said you were going off in that boat with Max Routlege.'

'I didn't know I was when I saw you,' said Abbie.

'Who else was on this trip?' asked Hugh.

When Abbie said, 'Nobody,' there was quite a long silence, then Hugh chuckled.

'I did say I'd hoped for something a bit livelier than the copy you wrote for us. Are we going to get something livelier?'

She laughed. It was small news to the big papers, but it would be quite a scoop for the *Penrann Telegraph* that local girl Leo Lansing's daughter, and Max Routlege who wrote best-sellers and TV hits, were getting married. She decided to give Hugh the date so that he could publish it first. Max wouldn't care, and she was sure her father would let her do the announcing. 'It's a promise,' she said.

She wrote to her father, trying to explain that she had found the man with whom she wanted to spend the rest of her life, without sounding too delirious. But she was so happy that the words came babbling instead of measured and reasonable. At last she wrote, 'As you told me all along the others were wrong, but Max is right I know.'

She posted her letter and busied herself with some of the mail that had arrived for her father during the week. She could still deal with his fan mail after she had married Max, but Maudie would be his problem when Abbie wasn't living at Players' Court. She said, 'When I go away, Maudie, we'll have to get someone in here full-time to give you a hand.'

'Don't bother your head about that,' said Maudie

promptly. 'If you love the man you marry him, if you're sure he can make you happy.'

'Oh, he can,' said Abbie. And she was sure she could make him happy too ...

Next day Abbie was cleaning out the drawing room, with the help of Audrey, when the phone rang. Audrey was dusting the little table on which an extension phone stood, and Abbie was running a polisher over the floor at the other end of the room. 'See who that is, would you?' said Abbie.

'Players' Court here,' Audrey announced, and then, 'It's Mr Lansing.'

Abbie whirled round so fast that she almost went skidding on the highly polished wooden blocks. She came running. 'Super!' she said, grabbing the phone from Audrey's outstreched hand.

Audrey backed discreetly away, but went on listening. This was interesting.

'Father,' said Abbie breathlessly. 'I'm so glad you rang. I've written to you, but it's lovely to hear your voice. Is everything all right? Is the film going all right?'

'So-so,' said Leo. 'Now, princess, what's all this about?'

'You mean Max?'

'Of course I mean Max. How did you come to be sailing with him all last week?'

'That's a long story,' said Abbie.

'Is it?' said Leo. 'I'm missing you, princess. Why don't you come over?'

Until now that would have had Abbie dashing to pack and make plane reservations. But today she said, 'I can't for a couple of days. As soon as Max comes back I will, but I have to wait for him.'

Fancy! thought Audrey, and catching Abbie's eye she blushed and very reluctantly left the room.

Then Abbie said, 'Father, you do like Max, don't you?'

'Why?' Leo demanded.

'Because,' she gulped and the words came in a little rush, 'we're going to get married.' She waited a few moments, then said, 'Father? Did you hear what I said?'

'Oh yes,' said Leo. 'Oh yes, I heard.'

'You're happy, aren't you? Please be happy, because I do love him so and I'm so very happy and——' her voice trailed away.

'Yes,' said Leo. 'Yes. Promise me something.'

'What?'

'Don't do anything rash until you've seen me and heard what I can tell you about Max Routlege.'

The air was feeling chilly around her, a creeping chill was on her skin. 'Can't you tell me now?' she pleaded.

'No,' said Leo. His breathing sounded laboured. 'I wish you were here, princess, I'm feeling my age.'

He had never said that before. He had complained of many ailments but never of age.

'I'll come as soon as I can,' said Abbie, 'but I wish you'd tell me what you've got against Max.'

'Have you told everyone you're marrying him?'

'Nobody yet. Except Maudie.'

'Then don't. Until you've seen me.'

'All right.' When Max came they'd go over and see her father together. Whatever her father had against him Max could answer, she was sure. 'All right,' she said again, and from a lifetime of caring for the genius who was her father she added, 'Don't worry, and you are taking all your pills, aren't you?'

She heard her father's sigh as he hung up, leaving her feeling guilty. Of course she was concerned about him. He had this heart condition, and the early days of a new play or film were always taxing without the additional stress of Abbie wanting to marry a man

147

about whom he had reservations. He was bound to have reservations. Max's eventful past was a good background for a writer, but a father might not approve of it all in a son-in-law.

But his past had made Max what he was, and that was how Abbie loved him, and no one could tell her anything that could turn her against Max.

She stood there, a few minutes longer, reassuring herself. At last she was able to go and tell Maudie, 'That was my father on the phone,' and sound quite cheerful about it.

'And?' said Maudie, screwing up her face.

'He wants me to go over. When Max comes we'll both go.'

Maudie's pursed lips and drawn-together eyebrows didn't relax, and Abbie went on very casually, 'What I told you, about Max and me getting married, have you told anyone else?'

'Ben,' said Maudie.

It was as well she hadn't mentioned it to Audrey, Abbie thought. Ben lived alone in his little house down in St Columb's, and he was the last to gossip. 'Because I've just promised not to broadcast it until I've seen my father,' Abbie said.

'I'll tell Ben.' Maudie looked as though she had a great deal more to say, and Abbie waited. But in the end Maudie said nothing, and went out into the gardens to look for Ben.

Abbie planned to be at the quayside early on the day Max would be sailing back. She would be sitting on that wall when the *Cormorant* came into harbour, if she had to take sandwiches and a flask of coffee and spend the best part of the day there. Even if it poured with rain.

It was a fine day, and she was too excited to eat breakfast. When the phone rang she answered it gaily, because she loved the whole world today. Except possibly Bryan, and it was him.

He was glad Abbie was back. He hoped she'd enjoyed her trip, and he was rather hurt that she hadn't told him she was going away.

She had no time for this. She took in a deep breath and said, 'Sorry, but I'm madly busy.'

'Abigail!' Bryan wailed in reproach.

'Who's she?' muttered Abbie. She said, 'You should keep your voice down at parties, you never know who's listening,' and hung up and left him to work that one out.

There was a man on the clifftop path. When she left the driveway of Players' Court there was a dark distant figure, coming towards her, and her heart lurched, and so did she, swaying on her feet. Then she began to run because it was Max, although he was too far away for her to distinguish features.

She ran and he walked, and she thought as she came closer—why isn't he running? But he was smiling and as she reached him he opened his arms and she fell into them, hard against him.

'I wanted to get down to the harbour,' she gasped. 'I wanted to be sitting on the wall again.'

'Why go back to square one?' said Max.

'Oh no. Only that little bit.' The world stopped when he kissed her. When it started again she said, 'Which way do we go now? Down to the *Cormorant* or up to the house?'

'The house,' he said.

They wouldn't be running a gamut of spectators that way, and there would be privacy in Players' Court. They could talk, be together, no one would walk in on them.

Abbie linked her arm in Max's and inquired, 'How did the business go?'

'As I expected.' Before she could ask if that was good

he asked, 'What's been happening with you?'

'Phone calls. Everyone saw that piece in the paper. You saw it?'

'Yes.'

'Not much else. I stayed here and waited for you.' She would tell him about her father's phone call when they were sitting quietly. Right now she only wanted to smile and hold his arm and feel the sun on her face and in her eyes. She wanted to savour happiness, and she brought him home, because home was where Max was: Players' Court, the *Cormorant*, the island, anywhere.

She took him to meet Ben in the garden, and into the kitchen to Maudie. Both Ben and Maudie looked serious, but Abbie hardly noticed, although when she and Max were alone she told him, 'Maudie likes you, she said so.'

'Good,' said Max. They were sitting on the settee in the drawing room, and she expected him to pull her into his arms, but instead he asked, 'Have you heard from your father?'

'Well, yes. Yes, I have.' She found she was smiling rather fixedly. 'You know how fathers are,' and that was a silly thing to say. 'Well, no, of course you don't.' She went on smiling. 'You don't, do you? You're not married or anything, are you?'

'What are you talking about?' said Max. 'You know I'm not.'

Of course she knew. She tried to make it droll. 'It's just that my father wants to talk to me about you. I expected a bit of a fuss, I suppose. I am his only daughter.' She grimaced, 'And you know what a sheltered life I've led, and he wants to be sure we know what we're doing.'

'As he always does,' said Max laconically.

Abbie sat in the middle of the sofa, leaning towards him, but he sat well back, arms crossed. 'I can tell you what your father's got against me,' he said. 'One thing. I want to marry you.'

'Why do you say——?' she began.

'I saw him yesterday.'

'That was your business? That was what you had to do before you asked me to marry you, get my father's permission?' It didn't seem Max's style. 'Wasn't that rather old-fashioned?' she said, puzzled.

'In this case,' said Max, 'it was a long shot, but necessary. And it might have worked.'

'What do you mean? What did he say?'

'That you wouldn't be happy with me.' As she began to protest he said, 'Nor I with you. You're a fragile lady who needs constant attention, and you spend money like water.'

'I am not, and I don't!'

'That's what the man said.' He didn't sound surprised. It was as though he had expected this kind of opposition from her father. 'You need luxury,' said Max. 'God, you're a mercenary wench, but he'll keep you if he can. Only it won't be for your sake. It will be for his.'

'No!' Her father had not spoken selfishly, she knew. He thought what he was saying was in Abbie's interests, and she said, sharply, 'That is not true. He's thinking of me. He thinks I need a sheltered life, and he's trying to protect me.'

'Every time?' Max drawled.

She stared. 'What?'

Anger was held back in his voice, she recognised that restraint. 'In one other case,' he said, 'I speak with certainty. If the others weren't dealt with in the same way perhaps there was bribery—King Leo is a powerful manipulator. But I'd stake my life they walked out on you on the direction of your father.'

Abbie's mind was whirling. She held her head, fingers

pressed to her temples, and started to laugh because he was talking such rubbish. Then she latched on to the perplexing thing he had just said and asked, 'What do you mean—one *other* case?'

'King Leo used the same script with Stephen Faber.'

'Stephen?' She blinked as though the room had gone hazy. 'Do you know Stephen?'

'Very well,' said Max, and while she tried to adjust to all that might mean, 'He believed you asked your father to get him out of your life.'

'*What?*'

'There was a party here that night, wasn't there? Early on your father took Stephen on one side and, all charm and sincerity, asked him to stop pestering you. Leo didn't give me that, but from then on it was much the same. Stephen was told what you considered your standard of living, and he agreed that he hadn't a hope of reaching it.'

She couldn't speak. She opened her mouth, but she could only gasp, and Max shrugged and said quietly, 'That was why I was prejudiced against you at the beginning. I took you on your father's valuation.'

'Stephen went off with another girl.' She got that out because that was what had happened. Maybe her father *had* talked to Stephen. Maybe her father *had* thought he was pestering Abbie, but Stephen had gone off with what-was-her-name and never phoned Abbie nor written to her. There had been no contact again after that goodbye.

'Her line was sympathy,' said Max cynically. 'Who do you reckon put her up to that? And you cleared off to Paris, and who took you there?'

Some time she must ask how Stephen was. Like now, while she tried to make some sense out of this. 'How is Stephen these days?' she said shakily. 'What's he doing with himself?'

'Still doctoring,' said Max.

'He was easily discouraged, wasn't he?' said Abbie.

'To him the brush-off seemed callous and final enough, so he got the hell out of here. He hoped for a while that you might get in touch.'

'*How?*'

'You could have done,' said Max.

From Stephen's holiday address? From things he had told her during their brief friendship? Yes, she could have done, but she had lacked the confidence, and she hadn't cared enough to risk greater hurt.

She said doggedly, 'My father was doing what he thought was best for me. Stephen didn't love me or he wouldn't have gone like that.' And I didn't love him or I wouldn't have let him go. 'But I love you,' she said, 'and why are you telling me this?'

'Because it's something you have to know,' said Max.

'All right, I know it. My father isn't over-anxious that I should get married. I know that, but I put a different interpretation on all this. I believe he's thinking of me, but are you saying——' The words stuck in her throat, she had to force them out. 'Are you saying you're not so sure you want to marry me after all?'

'I want to marry you.' But he still sat, arms folded. 'Your father's said all he can to me. And he knows he can't buy me off nor put me off.'

Max needed no favours, and an ostentatious display of wealth wouldn't impress or depress him, although she wouldn't accept that her father had used such tactics.

'He got rid of your other men,' Max said grimly, 'but this time the onus will be on you.'

Her lips were dry when she pressed them together, as Max said, 'I thought I might have a rival, and I have. Your father.'

She had imagined Max was jealous of Bryan, although it had seemed ridiculous, but it would be appalling if he resented her father, and she asked huskily, 'Can't I have a husband and a father?'

He laughed shortly. 'Try telling him that!'

It must have been a bad meeting. If only Max hadn't gone alone to see her father. He should have taken her —or at least told her what he was planning—because she was the one being discussed, the bone of contention.

She sighed and asked, 'What do you want me to do?'

'Marry me,' said Max.

'Yes, of course.'

'When?'

'As soon as you like.' More than anything she loved Max and wanted to marry him, but she did want her father to be happy for them, and he would be just as soon as she had seen him and talked to him. She began to smile, hoping to coax Max into smiling too.

'But I did promise not to make any announcements until I've seen my father.' Her voice quickened pleadingly. 'Look, it's going to be all right. Nothing can make any difference to the way I feel about you, and I know I don't need his permission, but I did promise, and whatever you think he has been a wonderful father to me.'

The shuttered look was on Max again. She could read nothing in his eyes and his face was like stone.

'He has.' She had thought Max was the most understanding man in the world, so how was it he couldn't accept something so obvious? 'You can't deny that he's given me a great deal. And not just material things; living with a genius has its advantages. There've been a few disadvantages, of course, but really they were trivial compared with——'

'Your father reduced and jeopardised you,' said Max harshly. 'He damaged and almost destroyed you.'

She shrank away, looking at him in a terror that was almost revulsion. 'No . . .' she whispered.

She was so firmly entrenched in her illusions that she must bitterly resent anyone who dragged her out and made her face reality, and Max said huskily, 'Oh God, I'm sorry.'

'You're wrong.' Abbie spoke through white lips.

He didn't answer that. He wasn't going back on what he had said, and there was a gulf, widening between them as they sat there, so that Abbie almost believed that soon he wouldn't hear her if she screamed.

The pain was like cramp. It paralysed her so that when she stretched out a hand she did it jerkily, and when Max reached for her she was stiff and resistant. Then she was in his arms, their mouths, then their bodies clinging together. Passion and urgency and delight rose in her like a warm wave, and she knew that he could make everything right for her for ever.

'I love you,' she whispered, with closed eyes and parted lips. 'Love me.'

'I love you,' said Max, his lips against her hair.

She opened her eyes. He still held her, strong and close and tender, but the control and the restraint were back and he smiled wryly. 'You know why I brought you back early from the island,' he said. 'You are the mots beautiful woman I have ever seen, and if you're going to walk out on me I've got all the memories I can handle.'

She could have laughed and cried. Her voice wobbled between tears and laughter. 'I could never walk out on you.'

He looked steadily at her, clear eyes in a hard face, and she almost said, 'If I did it wouldn't kill you, would it? No sea of desire is going to overwhelm you.'

She hadn't wanted to think, just to feel, but now she had to act rationally. She shrugged and asked, 'So what do we do now? Sail? Go walking? Should you be working?'

'What do you want to do?' he asked.

She wanted to be with him. She had thought they would stay here today, and Max would not have had to ask, 'What do you want?' He would have known she wanted him to love her, to be with her.

She had almost forgotten for the moment what he had said about her father, but now it came back, and with it her distress and resentment—less hysterical this time, but there was a gut reaction. He said, 'Shall we hit the road and see what turns up?'

'Why not?' She went upstairs to get her handbag, and paused, looking down at the pebbles on the dressing table. She had been going to give them to Max today, so that he could have her bracelet made. Not today, she decided. Another day.

They went driving, taking her car and the coast road. They ate at a little pub and on the surface they had a pleasant time. Her father's name was avoided as an area of pain, and Max's wooing was light, almost casual.

She supposed he was wooing her. He was complimentary, he made her laugh, he was the best of company; and she was being as gay as she could.

'You are the most beautiful woman I have ever seen,' he had just told her. She was no beauty, but she might have felt beautiful if anxiety hadn't been gnawing at her, remembering what he had said about her father.

Maudie came into the hall as they came back into the house. She looked worried and perplexed and as Abbie asked, 'What's the matter?' she handed her the cablegram.

It was from Richard Verney her father's agent. It said Leo Lansing was ill. It said that Abbie should get over there.

The shock was half expected. Abbie had always dreaded that he might have a heart attack, and yesterday's scene with Max had triggered one. She felt she had known it would.

She was consumed with guilt and fear, shaken to the core. She looked around wildly. 'I must go to him.'

Max read the cable and for a moment she thought he

was going to laugh. 'But of course you must,' he said. There was sardonic amusement in his voice, his expression was wholly cynical, and Abbie wondered if she was beginning to hate him.

CHAPTER EIGHT

ABBIE could have managed on her own, but Max took over and she didn't protest. He knew how to get a plane to get her to her father with the minimum of delay, and when he offered she was so worried that she just said 'Thank you' and went upstairs and started to pack.

Maudie followed her, and as Abbie took down a case with trembling hands Maudie said, 'This is just to scare you, there's nothing wrong with him, except he's bone selfish.'

That was a rough kind of comfort, Abbie supposed, but automatically she protested, 'He isn't selfish,' and Maudie said,

'Come off it, chicken. There isn't a more selfish man alive.'

Maudie had never said that before. She had always known it but had never said it, and in any case Abbie wasn't really listening to her.

Abbie had no doubts that her father was genuinely ill, nor that the scene with Max had been at least a contributing factor. The only way she could stop herself bursting into accusations was to say nothing.

She stayed in her room for a long time and then she said she wanted to be alone, and went into the gardens and walked to the cliff's edge, back and forth.

When Max came out of the house she waited, looking at him as though he was a stranger, and he said, 'I've spoken to Verney.'

'You phoned?' Of course he'd phoned.

'Your father isn't dying,' he said. 'He's filming.'

She had thought he was dying. She had thought she would reach him too late. She could still hardly believe it and she stared at Max, closely, suspiciously. 'Are you sure you phoned?' Then she coloured. 'Sorry, and I'm very grateful.'

Tears came then, sliding down her cheeks, but he made no move to dry them for her. He said, 'You'll want a plane, of course?'

She nodded. Leo Lansing would carry on with his work even if he was ill, and Dick had said Abbie should come, that her father needed her. Her father might still be working, but she was still worried, and Max was the last man to sympathise with that.

She turned away, staring out to sea, not even seeing the *Cormorant*, staring across the waves as though she could pierce the miles and reach the place where her father was.

Maudie came out after a while. Abbie was pacing the lawns nearer the house now, and when Maudie reached her Abbie said, 'He's still filming.'

'Of course he is,' said Maudie, although there was no 'of course' about it.

'Is—Max still here?'

'In the kitchen, talking to Ben.' Maudie placed herself so that they stood face to face and Abbie more or less had to listen. 'Before you go,' she said, 'I can tell you your father won't have you marrying Mr Routlege, or anybody else, if he can help it.'

'Why do you say that?'

'Because your father's all for number one. He wants you to spend your life looking after him.'

'He wants me to be happy.' Abbie's lips were trembling, but she spoke firmly, and Maudie flung back her grey head in soundless scornful laughter.

'He wants you to be where he can pick up a telephone and you'll answer every time.'

'Why not? He loves me. I'm his——' She had been going to say, 'I'm his daughter,' but Maudie snatched at that like a cue.

'His princess? More like his slave.'

'He doesn't even know I do any work, does he?' Abbie's eyes flashed angrily. 'He thinks I live the life of Riley.'

'If he'd known I wasn't up to doing all the housework and the cooking he'd have seen me off years ago,' Maudie announced dourly, and then it was Abbie's turn for scorn.

'Of course he wouldn't. He'd have got in some more help.'

'I know what he'd have done, and he wouldn't have thought twice about it.' Maudie's wrinkled face was scowling like a scolding witch. 'Nobody thinks more of your father than I do.' Her voice rose shriller. 'Like your mother he's one in a million, but so is Mr Routlege, I should have thought, and he's still a man you could turn to in trouble, and you're being a fool to him and to yourself.'

'Maudie, please don't make me quarrel with you,' Abbie begged desperately, and Maudie's voice dropped.

'You've quarrelled with Mr Routlege, haven't you?'

'No. Yes. I don't know. I don't know what's happening, except that I'm worried sick and I will be until I see my father, so please, Maudie, shut up!'

Abbie went past Maudie, round to the front door of the house, out of sight of the kitchen window. The furniture from the study was stacked in the hall and she took one of her scrapbooks of her father out of the desk and slipped into the drawing room, closing the door behind her, sitting down in the first deep easy chair.

When she turned the leaves of the scrapbook she could relive Leo Lansing's triumphs and her own small share in them. She was on some of the photographs, the grave smooth-haired girl that had been Abigail. She had been caught in King Leo's glamour all her life, and now she turned the pages feverishly as though she was trying to build up that unquestioning adoration again.

She heard the movement at the other end of the room, and looked up at Max, who must have been standing at a window when she came in, and who had been watching her for the last few minutes. She closed the book and said unnecessarily, 'I didn't see you.'

He could see what the book was, but he didn't comment on it. He said, 'We should be getting along to the airfield.'

'*We?*' She was not sure that Max should come. She faltered, 'I could manage, I don't need——' and he said dryly,

'You don't need me? Nevertheless I'll come. You know what writers are. It could be good copy.' When he reached her chair he stopped and she got up, clutching the scrapbook so that her knuckles whitened.

'It must be a comfort to know that no experience will be wasted,' she said, brittle and smiling, wondering if she was hurting him as much as he was hurting her.

She didn't want to say any more, it was best to be quiet. She went, looking pale but composed, and Max did everything. He stacked her cases in the boot, and got behind the wheel of the car.

He turned on the radio, filling the silence between them as they drove to the private airfield, and when they reached there Max dealt with all the formalities, putting her into her seat in the plane as though she was a child in his care.

He did almost all the talking there was, but none of it was personal. He could have been a travelling companion she was meeting for the first time. At the end of the flight she would have known nothing that mattered about him, except that he had charm and didn't lose. The things you only had to look at him to know.

But of course she knew so very much more than that. He was like her father, and yet so different. Both were men in a million, but in trouble, as Maudie had said, you would turn to Max. Abbie remembered the feel of his arms, comforting and holding her as her father never had, the light touch of healing fingers, his voice on the western peak when he had thought she was afraid.

She turned the memories of Max in her mind, like the leaves of the scrapbook, and she wanted to tell him she loved him and ask him to comfort her now, but he was too distant, too self-contained. She couldn't tell him she was terrified what they would find at their journey's end, although he must know that she was.

They phoned for more news as soon as they touched down on French soil, getting Richard Verney again, who had been expecting their call.

Max spoke to him first, nodding at what he heard, 'Yes . . . yes, all right,' and then handing the receiver to Abbie who was holding her breath beside him. 'How is he?' she asked for herself, and Verney said,

'He'll be fine, now you're here.'

There was a car waiting and Max was driving again, and Abbie tried to tell him she was grateful, but he shrugged off her thanks as though he would have done the same for any friend—which he probably would. Just as soon as she had seen her father, and reassured herself about him, she would devote every scrap of her time to breaking down this barrier between herself and Max. But, for now, she was too tense to talk, or even put her hand on his arm. She sat huddled in her seat, pretending to watch the scenery slipping by the car windows.

It was a short journey. Soon they came into the heart of the small town of Petit Limoges, which was post-card-pretty with its cobbled square and fountain, surrounded by tall houses interspersed with an inn, a few shops, and a couple of cafés spilling white chairs and tables on to the pavement.

The pointed towers of the château rose above the houses, but Max drove under the archway beside the inn, and as Abbie turned inquiringly told her, 'I'm staying here.'

'Yes.' That would be best, although surely he could have set her down at the château before he booked himself into the inn.

He said, 'Richard Verney will take you along. You wanted me to keep out of sight, didn't you?'

'I suppose so.' Abbie felt a little ashamed saying that. She was proud of having Max beside her, what woman wouldn't be? But after yesterday she should see her father alone first. All the same, asking Max to skulk in the shadows might be galling to his pride. She said, 'I'd better see him alone first, hadn't I? and then——'

'Of course you had.' He grinned. 'I had my audience with the king yesterday,' and although she could have wished he'd sounded less flippant at least he didn't sound offended. Almost as though it wasn't important, and perhaps it wasn't. Max had a certainty in himself that put him beyond touchiness.

He got out of the car, and Abbie followed him although he hadn't suggested she should, or for that matter told her to stay where she was. So she stood around in the shadowy hall, with whitewashed walls and red flagstones, while Max signed a register, and then led her to a settle in a bar and put a drink in front of her.

She was holding the glass, she had drunk a little although she couldn't have said afterwards what it was, when Richard Verney appeared in the doorway, and she jumped up so quickly that she sent most of her drink splashing. Max took the glass from her fingers, and Richard Verney smiled at them both.

'Good to see you,' said Richard approvingly. 'You didn't waste much time.'

'Max got me here,' said Abbie. 'I'm afraid I've been in rather a state.'

'Sorry, but I thought you should know he was a shade under the weather. He'll be glad to see you.'

'Run along,' said Max.

'You're staying here?' She had just seen him book in and he had told her he was, but she needed the reassurance of an agreed plan. 'I'll go and see my father and then I'll come right back,' she promised. 'You will be here?'

'Sure,' said Max.

If Richard had not been watching she would have kissed Max goodbye. She would have put her arms around him and said, 'Remember I love you.' But Dicky was watching, and Max moved away, and she knew it was because there was no tenderness in Max's face that she couldn't go to him and remind him she loved him. If there had been tenderness she wouldn't have cared who was watching.

'Goodbye,' she said.

As she walked along beside Richard Verney, down the road from the square leading to the château, she asked him about her father. She learned that Leo had been unwell last night, and although he was still keeping to his filming schedule Richard was concerned. She didn't probe any further, and they talked generalities for the rest of the way.

Any other time she would have thought that the château was very pretty. They passed through scrolled iron gates, bearing shields with coats of arms, down a tree-lined drive to the château; that was like a fairytale illustration, round pointed towers and curtained battlements reflected in the water of a moat.

Some of the rooms were production offices, some were being used as studios, and in some of them most of the company lived. Leo Lansing had a small suite, and Richard Verney took Abbie up to it by a back staircase, causing as little stir as possible.

She knew some of the company, but his aim was to

get her to her father without wasting time on the way. Last night Leo had told Richard that he wanted Abigail here. The bait, that Leo was unwell, had not been invention on Richard's part. Leo had been looking ragged enough to worry his agent, to whom Leo Lansing was a star client.

Leo was alone now, in his Louis-Quinze sitting room, with a hardly touched meal beside him, and a bottle of white wine from which he was on his second glass.

When Abbie walked in with Verney he gave her a weary, loving smile. 'Hello, princess,' he said, and there was a catch in his voice.

He looked too tired to rise. He lifted his hands and then let them fall heavily on the arms of the white-and-gold painted armchair, and Abbie ran across to him, and went down on her knees in the thick carpet, asking anxiously, 'How are you? I've been dreadfully worried.'

She searched his face, and saw strain and pain bravely borne and believed them, forgetting he was an actor, only remembering the ailing heart. Richard Verney left them, and as the door closed Leo asked, 'You haven't brought Max Routlege?'

'He came with me. He's staying in the village.' Leo scowled and quickly put a hand before his eyes, so that Abbie asked solicitously, '*Are* you all right?'

Leo met her gaze of deep concern with the brave smile again. 'I am now. Sit down, and——' he indicated the tray.

'I'm not hungry. I've been so worried about you.' She sat on a petit-point stool at his feet, looking up at him, and he said gravely,

'I've been worried about you too, princess. Very concerned. I still am.'

That was why he was ill, and she had to reassure him. 'What happened yesterday when Max came to see you?' she asked. 'What do you have against him?'

'He isn't the right one, princess. Any of the others would have been better for you.' Leo shook his head slowly and solemnly to stress the weight of that pronouncement, and Abbie said simply,

'He is right.' In everything but the enmity between the two men she loved.

'Listen to me,' said her father. So she listened, sitting quietly while Leo talked about Max Routlege, but as she listened she had to make an effort to control herself or she would have started to laugh.

Her father's case against Max was surely every woman he had ever set eyes on, but Max was no womaniser, Abbie knew that for sure; his nomadic way of life, travelling the world at whim, and what was wrong with that? Some of the tough spots he had got himself into—and out of, and which Abbie found more exciting than daunting.

When Leo said, as though it was the ultimate deterrent, 'He's a hard man, he's lived hard,' she said mildly,

'Father, I'm hard myself, I'm tough. Haven't you ever realised that?'

There was something in her manner that warned him she had become less manageable. He had never anticipated Abbie making a stand against him. Even when Max Routlege turned up yesterday, and said he wanted to marry her, Leo had still believed he could scotch that as soon as he got Abbie here.

Now he asked querulously, 'Is it a fact you've been doing most of the cooking and cleaning at home for years?'

'Max told you?' No one else knew, so it had to be Max.

Leo looked at her with reproach. 'You should have told me.'

'I enjoyed it,' said Abbie. 'It gave me something to do. I don't call that toughness. I mean I'm attuned to Max, we are right for each other. He's brilliant and yet I can talk his language.' And then she began to talk about Max, rather as she had written in the letter Leo would receive next morning, which would give him no comfort whatever.

She talked about Max's work, about the new book he would be starting to write any day. She said that none of the other men she had known had come anywhere near Max in any way, and that she knew that with just a little give and take he and her father must like each other. She teased happily, 'Wouldn't you rather have a famous son-in-law than one, like Bryan, who'll never amount to anything, you said?' and Leo asked abruptly,

'Will you wait six months?'

'Why?' When he didn't answer she said, 'Six months will make no difference.'

'I'm being selfish.' Leo sounded astonished, as though selfishness was quite alien to his nature. 'I'm thinking of myself. It will give me time to adjust to being without you.'

'You won't be without me.' She wouldn't be on such constant call, of course, but she wouldn't be too far away, the world wasn't that big; and she would always love her father and do everything she could for him.

'But I will be without you,' said Leo heavily. 'He intends to keep us apart, and that's going to break my heart.'

His expression of sorrow suddenly contorted as though with savage pain. He clutched the arms of the chair, fighting for breath that came in rattling gasps as Abbie scrambled to her feet, taking his hand and feeling it shaking in her hand.

She cried, 'I'll get someone,' but he held on to her, croaking,

'No need. No fuss. It's nothing—it's passing.'

He looked horrifyingly old and ill. His face was dragged into deep lines, and the smile he managed was a pathetic twitching travesty of Leo Lansing's famous smile.

As he fumbled in his inner pocket Abbie found the little packet of white 'panic pills' and shook out a couple, which he downed with a gulp of wine.

His forehead was wet with perspiration and she was still going for help as soon as she dared leave him. Leo sat back now in his chair, still gasping but still smiling, his eyes fixed on her, and she watched the clenched facial muscles relaxing, the breathing becoming easier. Then he said hoarsely, 'Sorry, princess.'

'I'm getting someone. You should be resting. You should——'

'*No*,' said Leo. 'We don't want everybody knowing I'm an old crock. It's tough enough at the top without a whisper getting around I could drop dead half way through the film.'

'Please don't talk like that.' It terrified her and he laughed.

'Don't look like that, princess, I'm not that bad. Just the odd twinge. I'm all right now.'

But there was still a whiteness around his lips. Abbie thought—he is not all right. One day this could happen and there could be no one to look after him; and she knew that she could not marry Max and go away until she had some assurance that she would be leaving her father safe.

'What were we talking about?' He sounded almost himself again and she said,

'Very well, we'll wait six months.'

'Ah yes.' He sounded as though, if she hadn't reminded him, he would have had difficulty recalling that request. 'Thank you,' he said.

'In the meantime,' said Abbie, 'you and Max can get to know each other,' and Leo, suddenly in fine humour, chuckled, 'Not while I'm working. I play a man who settles most of his problems by putting out an execution contract.'

'Not funny,' said Abbie, but she was glad to see the sparkle back in his eyes.

Leo took it for granted that she would be staying at the château, and when she said, 'I told Max I'd go back to the inn as soon as I'd seen you,' Leo said, 'Oh.'

'I don't know where I'll be staying until I've seen him.'

'That's up to you, of course,' said Leo. 'But I'd hoped to see something of you while you were here.'

'Well, you will,' said Abbie. 'That's why I've come, isn't it, to be with you?' and Leo said,

'Of course it is, princess, of course it is.'

He walked to the gate with her, so that now everyone knew that Abigail Lansing was here to watch her father filming. Most of them found it a matter of complete uninterest, although there were plenty of smiles and waves and hearty hellos.

'Did Max come up here?' Abbie asked, and Leo said,

'He does have some discretion. He sent me a note, I went down to the hotel to see him.'

That must have been very cloak-and-dagger, but she knew that her father wanted as little publicity about this as possible. She said, 'Doesn't anyone know that Max and I are marrying?'

'Not from me,' said Leo. 'And if you take my advice, princess, you'll stick to the just-good-friends routine if the reporters get on to you.'

He kissed her goodbye, and watched her go down the darkening street. Retracing his steps, he gave the gateman a gracious smile, and began to hum jauntily to himself. He felt he had just delivered a first-class performance.

The inn was half-timbered, with heavily weathered limestone and beams black with age. Abbie went in through the front door this time, but Max wasn't in the entrance hall, nor in the bar where she had left him, and the woman who had been watching behind a counter told her that Monsieur Routlege's room was number six on the first floor, and stretched out a hand to a phone to call him.

'I'll go up,' said Abbie. There were too many people about, she wanted to talk to Max in privacy.

The woman shrugged, picked up the phone and informed room six that a lady caller would be arriving.

Max opened the door as Abbie came up the stairs and into a narrow passage. She had been walking slowly, trying to decide how to tell him what had happened, but when she saw him her heart leaped and she fled into his arms as though she was magnetised. She clung to him desperately for a moment, breathing in the dear clean man-smell of his skin and hair, the comfortable aroma of his jacket. Then she looked up at him and he said, 'I gather there's talking to be done.'

'Yes. Some.'

'Come in.'

They went into the bedroom. It was a good-sized room, with a couple of chairs and a table set in a window alcove. You could breakfast there, Abbie thought, overlooking the square; or sit and have supper and watch the lights in the cafés and the people. Lights were starting to go on, but Max hadn't turned any on in here yet. The bed was large and dark behind her in the shadows, and when he pressed the light switch she blinked briefly.

It was discreet bedroom lighting, a couple of wall lamps, a lamp on the bedside table where the phone was, another on the little table in the window, but she realised that she would rather have sat in the shadows.

She said right away, 'I've promised to wait six months.'

'Wait six months for what?' said Max. Abbie felt he was laughing at her and felt the colour in her cheeks and said quietly,

'Before I go away. Before we—marry?' She made that a query.

'All right,' he said. 'Six months.'

It wasn't long, but she would have been happier if he had shown some impatience. He seated himself in one of the chairs in the window alcove, and she crossed the room and sat at the other, facing him. He was waiting for her to go on and she said impulsively, 'I wish you hadn't said about Maudie not being able to cope.'

'As I was being told you couldn't it seemed apposite to mention you'd been coping for years,' he drawled. 'Anything else?'

'He *is* ill, you know.'

A corner of Max's long mouth lifted and an eyebrow quirked in silent scepticism, and Abbie said desperately, 'He has a weak heart. He shouldn't be upset.' Still he said nothing and she burst out, 'Would you die if I left you?'

'No.' He didn't have to think about that. He needed nobody that much.

'My father could,' she said. 'He very well could.' She clasped her hands together, locking them and holding them tight against her. 'Why don't you help me,' she said in a tight little voice, 'instead of——'

'What do you want me to do?' Max cut in, and she told him,

'I want you to try to understand my father. He's a great actor. And he's a good father,' whatever Max thought. 'And he is ill,' again whether Max believed it or not.

'And he wants us to wait six months,' said Max. 'You'll stay with him that six months, of course?'

'More or less, yes.'

'He'll keep you close,' said Max grimly. Not close for

happiness but confined, locked in. That was what Max meant, and she was being torn apart. Neither man understood, neither would try to understand.

Her suitcase was on the floor over there. She looked at it and then at Max and asked, 'Do you want me to stay here?'

'And risk him having a heart attack in the middle of the night?' he said drily. 'You'd better get back before he does.'

That was a callous thing to say, that was unnecessary. 'All right,' she said. 'Goodnight, then.'

Max stood up as she did, and she asked, 'Do we kiss or shake hands?' He could at least have said that he wanted her to stay at the inn instead of the château. He need not have told her to get back as soon as she arrived. However this turned out he'd shed no tears. If she hadn't challenged him she doubted if he would even have kissed her, and she expected the kiss to be brief.

It was brief. He reached her in a couple of strides and held her, with an expression more of anger than love. His nearness made her shiver, and then his mouth was on hers and for that moment warmth wrapped her. She did not know who drew apart, perhaps she did, but her throat ached with tears.

Max looked down at her, without speaking, and she whispered, 'Will you be around at the end of six months?'

'Oh yes,' he said. But how? she wondered. Loving her still? Still wanting her? He picked up her small case and held the door into the hallway open for her.

They didn't talk. Abbie had to hurry to keep pace with his stride. She did ask, as they neared the scrolled iron gates, 'If the press get on to us what do we say?' and Max said,

'There's nothing to say.'

'I suppose not.' Did he mean nothing that was not

their own private concern? Or did he mean—nothing? He had called her that once, and she remembered the emptiness of it.

At the gate he handed her her case, looking down the drive to the château, more fairy palace than ever now that night was falling, and said, 'Remember me to Prospero.'

He was gone before she could call him Caliban, or do anything to pretend she thought he was joking. She walked alone to the château with a heavy heart.

There was not much night life around Petit Limoges, and the film schedule was rigid and arduous. Few of those engaged on it had the energy to go seeking entertainment in the evenings, so they stayed in the château, and tonight Leo Lansing had invited those who knew Abigail up to his salon, and laid in a good stock of wine.

It was like countless other evenings had been for Abbie. Her father, with his friends and colleagues, herself sitting near and saying little. Tonight she observed with a more ironic eye and felt more detached, because she now had a vital life of her own, but she was quite interested in their professional chat, and then—inevitably—Max Routlege's name came up.

Corinne, was here, of course. Corinne had been very surprised that Abigail had gone sailing away with Max Routlege, because at that dinner party at Players' Court they hadn't seemed to hit it off at all. So almost as soon as she came into the room Corinne was asking, 'How's Max? I suppose he isn't here?' looking hopefully around.

Before Abbie could speak Leo said, 'As a matter of fact Max did come over with Abigail, but he's working, writing.'

They knew Max's work, and they discussed it. A couple of the actors had played in Max's TV plays and they said that the roles had been a joy. And then Leo took over.

At first Abbie was glad that her father's professional appreciation seemed to be so generous. Max was a friend of his, he insisted, as much as of Abbie's. He played down the romantic aspect, but she had expected that and she didn't contradict, and he was almost lyrical about Max's work.

'This book he's starting to write,' said Leo expansively, 'that is going to make a memorable film,' and as Abbie leaned warningly forward he began to tell them all about it; the plot, the twists, the climax, overriding Abbie's protests, the born raconteur with his teeth into a good tale.

Short of shrieking, 'Be quiet, you fool!' she could see no way of stopping him. And that would have sharpened everyone's interest with a vengeance. She could only pray they'd all forget what they'd heard, but there were scriptwriters here and PR personnel, and Max's wonderful book, that was still in his head, had been given a thorough airing.

She was so angry herself that she waited five minutes more, hoping no one would link cause with effect, and then said, 'I'm tired, I've had a long day. I think I'll go to bed.'

They had put up a bed for her in a tiny dressing room, off a room shared by Corinne and one of the make-up girls. As she tried to sleep Abbie decided that she was the one who had been imprudent. She shouldn't have discussed Max's next work with anybody. Her father probably thought he was doing Max a good turn, advertising his book in advance, stressing its film potential.

She must get down to the inn early in the morning and explain to Max, or he could easily meet someone and hear from them how Leo had entertained half the company last night.

Work started early in the château. Everyone was up

and about when Abbie went, breakfastless, through the iron gates and into the streets of Petit Limoges. Shops were beginning to open in the square, but the front of the inn was shuttered, and she had to go round to the back and knock on a door that stood a little ajar.

She was answered at once by a man in shirt-sleeves, with a dark blue apron tied round his waist, and when she said who she wanted to see he gestured her in. Monsieur Routlege was in the dining room, he told her, the dining room was down there and to the right.

'Thank you,' said Abbie, and followed his directions.

Half a dozen tables were laid for breakfast. Two near the door were occupied, and Max sat behind a French newspaper at the far end of the room. He would have heard her coming, the whole of the ground floor was flagstoned with the occasional rug, and it seemed to her that her footsteps made a great clatter, although she was trying to walk quietly.

He put down his paper when she was nearly at his table and smiled, but it was an inquiring grin. Abbie must have been looking anxious because he said, 'Hello, what's happened now?'

'Good morning.' She sat down and nodded, 'Please,' when he suggested, 'Coffee?'

He signalled to a waitress and until the girl brought another cup and another pot Abbie talked about the film. She needed a drink, she hadn't even had a drink this morning, and she sipped a little of the dark hot strong liquid before she said, 'Something has happened, and it's my fault and I'm very sorry.'

'Sorry for what?'

'I told my father about your new book, and last night he started to talk about it. He said it was going to make a marvellous film, and he told a few of them the plot.'

Max swore softly.

'I am sorry,' she said.

'That settles one thing,' he said. 'I'd better get the bloody book written instead of hanging around here wasting time.'

Wasting time hanging around her? She said quietly, 'You couldn't write here, I suppose?'

'No.' He was adamant on that. 'You're staying here, of course?'

'I have to, for a while. Where will you go?'

'Back to London, probably.' To the flat overlooking the Thames.

'When?'

'Today.'

She had known he wouldn't be 'hanging around here' long, but she hadn't thought to lose him so soon, and she couldn't plead with him to stay. He had to get down to work, especially now she had announced his forthcoming book in detail. She said, 'I won't be here very long myself.' She would leave just as soon as she was sure that her father was fit again. 'A week or so, I should think,' she said.

'And then?'

'Back to Players' Court.'

He wrote a London phone number on a scrap of paper from his wallet, and Abbie looked at it, memorising it, seized with an irrational dread that she might lose it and not be able to trace him. As though links were snapping all the time. She apologised again, 'I'm sorry about the book.'

'No matter,' he said. But he glanced at his watch as though he was anxious to be on his way, and although her cup of coffee was still half full she heard herself say,

'I'll leave you, then. You'll have things to do.'

She could have stayed with him while he phoned. She could have driven with him to whichever airport he was leaving from, but he was probably still annoyed at her babbling about the book because he said, 'That's right.'

Then he got up from the table, so that she had to get up too. In the hall he said, 'Phone me when you're coming back,' and went to the phone booth in the corner.

'Goodbye,' she said to his back, and Max turned and gave her a half wave.

Abbie walked slowly all around the square before she made her way to the château. Nothing had changed, she told herself. Max loved her and she loved him. Perhaps she loved more, but it would still work out because it had to.

When she got back the château was a hive of industry. Everyone else was busy as bees, but she was a drone and there was nothing for her to do. She watched her father at work for a little while, in the great white and gold salon, transformed into a studio, where most of the interior shooting took place.

'He's been asking after you,' several people had told her, and between shots Leo strolled across, smiling.

'Hello, princess, I thought you'd gone off for the day.'

No one was listening to them, and Abbie told him what he wanted to hear. 'Max has gone.'

'So soon?'

She sighed. 'I do wish you hadn't told them all about the plot of his new book last night. He told it to me in confidence, and he didn't need it broadcasting at this stage.'

'So I betrayed a confidence?' Leo sighed even deeper than Abbie had sighed. 'I had no idea, but of course I should have realised. Routlege knows about this?'

'That's why he's gone. To get down to work.'

'Annoyed, was he?'

'Of course he was.'

'My humble apologies, princess.'

She quoted Max, 'No matter,' and Leo was called back to take his place in front of the cameras, where he slipped into the role he was playing, immediately and brilliantly.

Abbie felt a cold sinking sensation in the pit of her stomach. She knew he had betrayed that confidence deliberately, to cause a rift between her and Max. He had been so pleased it had worked that the glee had shown under his protestations of regret.

He made no secret that he didn't want Abbie to marry Max, but that had been a mean little trick. A man who would play a trick like that could have told Stephen that Abbie had complained he was pestering her.

She had put up a solid disbelieving front against the things that Max, and Maudie, had said yesterday about her father. But this small thing she saw with her own eyes, and this was a hair crack that widened.

'He'll keep you if he can,' Max had said. 'But it won't be for your sake, it will be for his own.' And at last Abbie was beginning to see the self-interest in the charm, the self-love that outweighed all other.

It was a bad time for her. Sometimes she wished she had stayed with her illusions. She had been on location with her father before and enjoyed herself, but she was not enjoying herself now, although this was the same old set-up.

Leo even had a new bracelet brought along for her. The company admired it, but when she was alone with him she said, 'You keep this somewhere safe. I'm not wearing so much jewellery these days. Besides,' she smiled a wry and knowing smile, 'I feel you should get it inscribed "In memory of Max", because that's what you hope it is, don't you? Another consolation prize.'

'I have no idea what you're talking about,' said Leo.

Abbie hadn't heard from Max, and as the days passed she became increasingly fearful about that. She tried several times to ring the number he had left her, but there was never a reply. He must have changed his mind about going to the flat, but he hadn't bothered to contact her with another number or another address.

Of course he was working, but he could still have found time to send a postcard. Unless this was the acid test, and he was leaving her alone to make up her mind, kill or cure, all or nothing. She would go looking for him soon, but it showed that he needed her less than she needed him. He could cut loose, without bleeding to death.

She was asked about Max constantly, and she could say with honesty that she had no idea where he was. Somewhere working, of course. Which was more than she was doing. Her father wanted her in the background while he was filming, the rest of the time he wanted her listening to him and ministering to him, and she was going crazy with boredom and frustration.

After nearly two weeks of it she could take no more. She was going back to Players' Court where she could at least find something constructive to do, and where she might see the *Cormorant* riding the waves in St Columb's Cove.

Her father seemed in excellent health again. He was giving a cracking performance in his current role, and basking in general approbation, although when Abbie told him she was returning to England he looked gloomy.

'I'll go and see how the builders have left the study,' she said.

That couldn't do much harm, he decided, and he could always get her back. 'Do just what you like, princess,' he said fondly. 'While you're there you might see about finding a new housekeeper, ring up the agencies and interview anyone who seems promising.'

'Yes, I will.'

'I'll be sorry to lose Maudie,' sighed Leo.

'Lose Maudie?' Abbie echoed.

'You'd better see about that too,' said Leo, brisk

again. 'Find out how much she'll be needing, and make the arrangements.'

He *was* going to pension Maudie off, and turn her out. Not while I'm in Players' Court, thought Abbie. And if I leave I'll make sure that Maudie has a happy home. 'I'll see to Maudie,' she said quietly.

She had written to Ben and Maudie, just saying she was here safe and sound, that it was a beautiful château, beautiful countryside. She hadn't mentioned Max, or anything really important. The important things would wait until she saw them.

She phoned that evening, but Maudie distrusted telephones. She always kept telephone talk short, and hung up if a caller paused for longer than three seconds. When Abbie asked if everything was all right Maudie said, 'Yes.'

'I'll be back tomorrow or the next day,' Abbie told her.

'Yes,' said Maudie.

It was a crackling line, and Abbie raised her voice to ask, 'Is the *Cormorant* there? Max's boat?'

'No.'

'Have you—seen it at all?'

'No.'

'Oh! Well, I'll make my own way from the airport, so expect me when you see me. By the way, my father's fine again now. He's quite well again.'

'Ha!' said Maudie, followed by a burst of atmospherics, during which they were either cut off or she hung up.

Abbie replaced her dead phone and remembered that when that cable had arrived Maudie had said, 'There's nothing wrong with him, except he's bone selfish.'

He was selfish enough to turn his back on a loyal old friend who had outlived her usefulness, and Abbie was dreading telling Maudie how right she had been.

She was looking at her father with clearer vision

these days, and not liking what she saw. She was even wondering if that weak heart of his could be a con trick. He had a doctor, whom he saw fairly regularly, but no one but Leo had ever told Abbie that his heart was at risk. It was all hush-hush, and it had proved a highly effective emotional blackmail to bring Abbie running and ready to promise him anything.

She had already decided that when she got back she would get in touch with their doctor. She would explain she was worried, and she was almost a hundred per cent certain he would confirm that there was nothing wrong with her father's heart. Nothing physically wrong, that is.

But she didn't have to ask the doctor. She got a moment more or less alone with Richard Verney when she said goodbye to him. 'I'm going back home tomorrow,' she said. 'My father's all right now, isn't he?'

'Top of his form,' said the agent enthusiastically. 'He's really into the skin of the part.'

'Yes. When you sent for me, there was nothing seriously wrong with him, was there?'

'Well——' He didn't want her to think he had summoned her for nothing. 'The artistic temperament, you know. He wanted you here, and he was feeling tired and rather depressed. His performance might have suffered if you hadn't come.'

She made it a direct question. 'He doesn't have a bad heart, does he?' and Richard Verney told her,

'Good lord, no, nothing like that. He has a thorough physical before any major film. He did before this one, and a clean bill. He's in great shape.' He smiled at Abbie, glad to reassure her, sure she shared his opinion of her father's talents. 'But you know what the big names are, they've got to be humoured.'

'Haven't they just?' said Abbie.

She had been blind as a child over her father, and she could have wept like a child. If Max had been there it wouldn't have been so bad. Nothing could have hurt her too badly if Max had been there.

She had no illusions left about her father. He was a great actor and, as Max had said, a great manipulator. No illusions about Max either. He was a man who loved her enough to want to marry her, but not enough to give himself unreservedly. Perhaps he never would, and she would be seeking and following all her life, even if they married.

Once she was back in England she could keep phoning the number he had given her. Or she could get a boat and go out to the island. She thought he must be at the island and, flying over the clouds over the Channel, she imagined herself sailing as near as she dared to the sharp white rocks that were like teeth, and Max on the *Cormorant* waving at her and coming for her.

She tried to tell herself it was a good dream, it would be lovely like that, but she knew it would mean that he could sail away without her, and stay away from her, and in the deepest recess of her mind she wondered if she had already lost him.

She took a taxi from the airport and by the time she reached St Columb's it was dark and she was cold. She paid off the taxi and carried her case up to the front door, ringing the bell and then putting her key in the lock so that Maudie came into the hall as Abbie stepped through the front door.

Maudie was expecting her, she had phoned when she landed. Maudie came fleet-footed, in spite of her arthritis, with anxious eyes that told Abbie she had guessed something of what had been going on in the château of Petit Limoges.

'The kettle's on,' said Maudie. 'Nice hot cup of tea?'
'Yes, please.'

There were letters on the Chinese chest in the hall, and Abbie went through them quickly, but none was in Max's handwriting. Nor was there a message from him on the notepad by the telephone. Later she would ask Maudie if she had heard anything from anywhere about Max, but now she had to bite her trembling lip, and when Maudie asked, 'What is it, chicken?' she couldn't talk about Max.

Instead she said, 'You were right about my father, but you mustn't worry. If I stay here no one will shift you, I promise you that, and if I do go I'll get you a little cottage. I thought in St Columb's, near to Ben.'

Maudie began to chuckle. 'That's funny,' she said. 'That's where I'm going. To Ben.'

Of course, Ben's cottage was big enough for two, and they had always got on so well together. 'I can just manage a little house,' said Maudie. 'And with you getting married I could see the writing on the wall here.'

'I'm glad,' said Abbie. 'I'll take my case up. I'll come straight down.'

When she got into her bedroom her case slipped from her nerveless fingers on to the floor. She had thought there would be a note, or message. She had pinned her hopes on that. That was the real reason she had come home.

But there was nothing, and she was afraid of nothingness. She knew what it meant. If Max had gone the loneliness would close in on her like heavy wings, blotting out everything.

She saw her white face and dark-shadowed eyes in the dressing-table mirror, and walked towards her reflection, trying desperately to hold back the tears. Reaching the dressing-table, she stood stock still. Then she opened the top drawer, closed it quickly and opened another.

But the pebbles had gone. She had left the tiny stones that were her memories of the island scattered on the top of the dressing-table, and Maudie—who never bothered about the room while Abbie was here—must have come in to deal with the dust that was gathering and seen the sea-shore pebbles and swept them away.

They were gone. They were in none of the drawers, and it was a crazy thing to prove the last straw, but it did. She yelled 'Maudie!' and ran to the top of the stairs, and Maudie, who had been slowly following her up, stood stock still, staring, asking, 'Whatever's the matter?'

'Where are my pebbles?' As she spoke Abbie thought how stupid that sounded. 'I left them on my dressing-table.'

'Oh, them. Mr Routlege took them,' said Maudie. 'He's having them made into a bracelet.' No accounting for tastes, said her expression, and the sun came out, brighter than all the electric lights, for Abbie.

'Has Max been here?'

'He is here,' said Maudie. 'You didn't give me a chance to tell you. He's in the drawing room.'

Abbie stopped for a second to hug Maudie, then plunged past her, down into the hall, and along to the closed door of the drawing room. Max was here, Maudie had just said so, but she still held her breath opening the door.

He was standing by the fireplace. He must have known Abbie was here. He would have heard the taxi and the doorbell, heard her in the hall, so why hadn't he come out into the hall? Why was he standing half a room's distance from the door?

And then she saw the uncertainty in his face, and knew that he was unsure of his welcome. 'Surprised?' he said.

She wasn't surprised. She had come home to Max, it was as simple as that.

'Are you glad to see me?' he asked, as though he thought she might not be glad, and she was stammering because there weren't the words to say how glad she was.

She ran to him. 'Yes, oh, yes, oh, very much yes!' as

she went into the arms that he folded around her, hungrily, fiercely. 'Why did you go?' she asked him. 'I know you were angry about the book, but——'

'I couldn't be angry with you about anything for longer than five minutes.' He took her across to the sofa, and she sat beside him, snuggling close. The last time they were together here he had sat, arms folded, self-contained. Now he held her as though he would never let her go.

'I thought I'd get on with some work while you were deciding if you wanted to spend the rest of your life in your father's shadow,' he said in his slow deep voice. 'How is he, by the way?'

'Acting superbly,' she said. 'Everybody says so. He bought me another bracelet, which I told him I didn't want. He's in fine form and very good health.' Max understood she was telling him he had been right about her father. She added wryly, 'He wouldn't die if I left him.'

'I would,' said Max. 'As soon as I was away from you the world dried up.' He looked at her as though that had been the literal truth. 'I don't know why I tried to fool myself I could let you walk away from me,' he said, 'because I can't.

'From that first day on the island when I saw you swimming across the cove I was heading for those rocks. Me. Part of me. You were already under my skin then, and the only way I could go on without you now would be to cut my heart out.' He grinned a little, but there was no laughter in it. 'Either way,' he said, 'without you I'm finished.'

She reached for him, pulling his face down to hers, kissing him with all her love and all her passionate young strength. Then her head fell back on his shoulder and she looked up at him. 'I like looking at you,' she said, and she put her fingertips here and there on his face, 'And I like touching you.'

'You took the words right out of my mouth.' He kissed her again, and she spoke against his lips,

'I tried to phone the flat, but there was never an answer. Why didn't you write to me?'

'I did.' He moved his head back a fraction and spoke clearer. 'I gave you a Salcombe number. I had the *Cormorant* there. When you never rang I phoned here each day, and yesterday Ben told me you were coming back.'

'I didn't get your letter, I suppose it's still on its way.' Letters were always getting delayed these days, and from Salcombe it had had a fair way to travel, but he said,

'Then it's taking more than fourteen days to get from Orly to Petit Limoges. I posted it at the airport the day I left.'

The same suspicion struck them both at the same time, that Leo had somehow intercepted.

'He *wouldn't*,' Abbie gasped.

'He would,' said Max, and this should have been the blackest disillusionment of all, proving that her father had no scruples and no pity. She could have been in touch with Max all along, and she could have been spared a great deal of heartache.

'Yes, he would,' she said. 'Oh, how wicked!'

But Max was smiling, and she realised that she was smiling too, and without bitterness. She said slowly, 'He is a shocker.' Not wicked, just a spoiled small boy, ferociously intent on getting his own way. 'I'll always love him,' she said. He was a lovable small boy. And talented. 'And he is a great actor, isn't he?'

'He is,' said Max. 'Shall I write him a play?'

'Yes, please. He'd like that.' One of Max's top-rating TV plays could melt her father's opposition entirely. In any case she knew enough of Leo Lansing now to know he would make a virtue of necessity, milk the situation for all the publicity he could, and play the proud father of the bride.

She would never see her letter, though, and she asked, 'What would you have said to me if I had phoned that Salcombe number?'

Max held her in the curve of his arm, and she closed her eyes, loving the sound of his voice. 'I can go nowhere without you,' he said. 'Let me bring the *Cormorant* and fetch you. Please come back to the island with me.'

'Is she in the cove?'

'Yes.'

Abbie opened her eyes, looking into his eyes.

'Dear Caliban,' she said, 'of course I'll go back to your island with you.'

To the magic island that had changed her life, and brought her a love that would last for ever.

'Oh God, I love you,' said Max huskily.

'When is the tide for sailing?'

'Around midnight.'

'Maudie made tea,' she said. 'It's going to be over-brewed, but we've time for a cup. I'll have to pack a few more clothes and then we'll tell her.'

It hurt to move out of Max's arms, but it wouldn't be for long. He stood with her, still holding her.

'I'm supposed to be finding a housekeeper for here,' she said. 'But it can wait. Did you know Maudie's going to live with Ben?'

Max grinned. 'I don't think she'd put it that way. She's going to marry Ben.'

'Is she?' Abbie goggled with astonishment. 'How do you know?'

'They told me.'

'Imagine that!' It was a splendid solution. They were perfect for each other. 'Imagine you knowing and not me.' She pretended to be offended and was delighted. She asked in mock huffiness, 'Is there anything you don't know?' and he drew her close, the whole length of her pressed against him, so that she could feel his heart beating, and her own slow sweet trembling at the touch of his lips and his hands.

'On what subject?' he asked, softly against her ear.

Smiling, she said, 'You do know it all, don't you?'

'What I don't know I'll learn, with you.'

'Yes, you will.'

'About Maudie——'

She steadied herself, bringing herself back to earth. 'Maybe she'll make us a fresh pot of tea, if we ask her nicely.'

'And you can tell her we're getting married in the next few days.'

Abbie shrugged, teasing, elaborately offhand. 'Why should I tell her? She didn't tell me she was marrying Ben.'

'She will.'

She pretended to think about it. 'All right. We'll go and tell her.'

In the open doorway to the hall they turned to look at each other. 'That you're marrying me,' said Max huskily.

She smiled at her husband, at her life and her love. 'And we're sailing with the tide,' she said.

Did you miss any of these exciting Harlequin Omnibus 3-in-1 volumes?

Each volume contains 3 great novels by one author for only $1.95.
See order coupon.

Violet Winspear

Violet Winspear #3
The Cazalet Bride (#1434)
Beloved Castaway (#1472)
The Castle of the Seven Lilacs (#1514)

Anne Mather

Anne Mather
Charlotte's Hurricane (#1487)
Lord of Zaracus (#1574)
The Reluctant Governess (#1600)

Anne Hampson

Anne Hampson #1
Unwary Heart (#1388)
Precious Waif (#1420)
The Autocrat of Melhurst (#1442)

Betty Neels

Betty Neels
Tempestuous April (#1441)
Damsel in Green (#1465)
Tulips for Augusta (#1529)

Essie Summers

Essie Summers #3
Summer in December (#1416)
The Bay of the Nightingales (#1445)
Return to Dragonshill (#1502)

Margaret Way

Margaret Way
King Country (#1470)
Blaze of Silk (#1500)
The Man from Bahl Bahla (#1530)

40 magnificent Omnibus volumes to choose from:

Great value in Reading!
Use the handy order form

Elizabeth Hoy
Snare the Wild Heart
(#992)
The Faithless One
(#1104)
Be More than Dreams
(#1286)

Roumelia Lane
House of the Winds
(#1262)
A Summer to Love
(#1280)
Sea of Zanj (#1338)

Margaret Malcolm
The Master of
Normanhurst (#1028)
The Man in Homespun
(#1140)
Meadowsweet (#1164)

Joyce Dingwell #2
The Timber Man (#917)
Project Sweetheart
(#964)
Greenfingers Farm
(#999)

Marjorie Norell
Nurse Madeline of Eden
Grove (#962)
Thank You, Nurse
Conway (#1097)
The Marriage of Doctor
Royle (#1177)

Anne Durham
New Doctor at
Northmoor (#1242)
Nurse Sally's Last
Chance (#1281)
Mann of the Medical
Wing (#1313)

Henrietta Reid
Reluctant Masquerad
(#1380)
Hunter's Moon (#1430)
The Black Delaney
(#1460)

Lucy Gillen
The Silver Fishes
(#1408)
Heir to Glen Ghyll
(#1450)
The Girl at Smuggler's
Rest (#1533)

Anne Hampson #2
When the Bough Breaks
(#1491)
Love Hath an Island
(#1522)
Stars of Spring (#1551)

Essie Summers #4
No Legacy for Lindsay
(#957)
No Orchids by Request
(#982)
Sweet Are the Ways
(#1015)

Mary Burchell #3
The Other Linding Girl
(#1431)
Girl with a Challenge
(#1455)
My Sister Celia (#1474)

Susan Barrie #2
Return to Tremarth
(#1359)
Night of the Singing
Birds (#1428)
Bride in Waiting
(#1526)

Violet Winspear #4
Desert Doctor (#921)
The Viking Stranger
(#1080)
The Tower of the Captive
(#1111)

Essie Summers #5
Heir to Windrush Hill
(#1055)
Rosalind Comes Home
(#1283)
Revolt — and Virginia
(#1348)

Doris E. Smith
To Sing Me Home
(#1427)
Seven of Magpies
(#1454)
Dear Deceiver (#1599)

Katrina Britt
Healer of Hearts
(#1393)
The Fabulous Island
(#1490)
A Spray of Edelweiss
(#1626)

Betty Neels #2
Sister Peters in
Amsterdam (#1361)
Nurse in Holland
(#1385)
Blow Hot — Blow Cold
(#1409)

Amanda Doyle #2
The Girl for Gillgong
(#1351)
The Year at Yattabilla
(#1448)
Kookaburra Dawn
(#1562)

Complete and mail this coupon today!